Esaias Tegnér, H Spalding

The Tale of Frithiof

Esaias Tegnér, H Spalding

The Tale of Frithiof

ISBN/EAN: 9783337070830

Printed in Europe, USA, Canada, Australia, Japan

Cover: Foto ©Andreas Hilbeck / pixelio.de

More available books at **www.hansebooks.com**

THE

TALE OF FRITHIOF.

BY

ESIAS TEGNER.

TRANSLATED FROM THE SWEDISH

By CAPT^{N.} H. SPALDING,

104th Fusiliers.

LONDON:

JOHN MURRAY, ALBEMARLE STREET.

1872.

PREFACE.

IN publishing this poem, the translator thinks it desirable to point out that his chief endeavour has been to adhere as closely as possible to the original, which is confessedly of surpassing beauty. The twenty-four sections into which the poem is divided are written each in a different measure. Some of these are peculiar : and this circumstance considerably increases the difficulty of giving a faithful and yet harmonious version. The translator has followed these measures without deviation, except in XXI., in which the alliteration has been abandoned from a fear of sacrificing the meaning of the context.

FORT GRANGE, GOSPORT.
May 3, 1872.

CONTENTS.

———◆———

CONTENTS.

FRITHIOFS SAGA.

FRITHIOF AND INGEBORG.

In the far North, mid verdure fair,
Two flowers bloomed, a lovely pair,
In Hilding's charge they there were nourished,
And gloriously they grew and flourished.

The one did like an oak arise,
That points its summit to the skies,
All trembling in the fitful gale
Like crest of warrior clad in mail.

The other, like the blushing rose,
When winter, still reluctant, goes ;
And spring, with many a zephyr light,
Brings the young blossom into sight.

The storm around the earth shall rage,
The oak shall with its warfare wage ;
But the spring sun shall lend its glow,
And open the red rose below.

So thus with joy their course they took,
And Frithiof was the stately oak ;
The rose that fragrant scents the air,
Her name was Ingeborg the fair.

Saw you the pair by midday beam,
In Freya's[1] Court yourself you'd deem,
Where many a little couple swings,
With golden hair and rosy wings.

But saw you them by moonlight sheen,
Dance round beneath the branches green,
You'd say that 'neath the spreading grove,
The elf king dances with his love.

How glad, how full of pride the boy
When first the rune[2] was spelt ; with joy
He hastened to his Ingborg fair,
And wished to teach her then and there.

Upon the dark blue deep his wherry
Glided with her so light and merry ;
How gladsome when the sail he veers
She claps her tiny hands and cheers !

No nest so difficult to reach
He climbed not from the pebbly beach.
The eagle, hovering in the air,
Lost eggs and young for Ingeborg fair.

No brook was found, how swift so e'er,
O'er which he could not Ingeborg bear ;
Who, frightened by the stream's alarms,
Clings to him with her small white arms.

The first young bud that spring brings forth,
The first red strawberry in the north;
The first young spike whose gold is red,
He brought to her so true and glad.

But childhood's days too soon are past,
The boy becomes a man at last,
Who onward pants with hope and prayer,
The girl becomes a maiden fair.

Young Frithiof dearly loved the chase,
But few would dare his sport to face,
For without blade and without spear
The bold boy seized a grizzly bear.

Thus, breast to breast, they struggled on,
The hunter, torn and bleeding, won,
And home he bore his shaggy prize ;
Could maid refuse to hear his sighs ?

Man's courage e'er is woman's boast ;
The brave deserve the fair the most ;
A maid is wont the brave to wed,
E'en as a helmet fits the head.

And many a winter's evening dire,
When seated by the great hall fire,
He sang of Valhalla[3], and told
Of gods and goddesses of old.

He sang : tho' yellow Freya's tresses
As cornfields which the wind distresses,
Fair Ingeborg's are like a net
Of gold round rose and lilies set.

Iduna's[4] breast is fair, I ween,
It beats beneath a silk of green ;
I know a silk, whose folds do hide
Two fairies bright on either side.

And Frigga's[5] eyes have that deep blue
Which shames the heaven's ethereal hue ;
I know two eyes, against them both
The spring day to compete was loath.

Why praise ye Gerda's[6] soft cheeks so,
Aurora on the new-fallen snow ?
I know two cheeks like rosy morn,
When night is chased by coming dawn.

I know a heart, which, soft as wax,
Not one of Nanna's[7] virtues lacks.
By poets art thou justly lauded,
Balder[8], by Nanna's love rewarded !

Oh, that my bones might thus be laid,
Bewept by my own peerless maid,
Who, soft and faithful, may compare,
Balder, to thine own Nanna fair.

The royal maiden sat and wove,
And sang a lay of war and love,
She wove the cloth with heroes bold,
Their deeds on sea and barren wold.

She wove them on a snow-white field,
With yellow wool the glittering shield,
The lance of combat flourished red,
And graced the silver helm each head.

But ah! she wove from day to day
Her hero Frithiof's features play,
And when they from the canvas blazed,
She blushed with joy, yet half amazed.

But Frithiof cut upon a beech
The letters I and F, till each
Constrained by time and growth and weather,
In faithful union grew together.

When day arose upon the sky,
Old Worldking, with the flaming eye,
And men began to move and stir,
She thought of him, and he of her.

When night upon the earth upstood,
Worldmother, with her starry brood,
When silence reigns and planets err,
She dreamed of him, and he of her.

"Thou Earth, who yearly dost adorn
Thy tresses green with flowers and corn,
Give me the best, that I may bear
A chaplet to my Frithiof dear."

"Thou deep blue sea, give up the pearl
From depths where darkling eddies whirl,
Give me the best, that I may make
A necklace for my Ingeborg's sake."

"Thou knob on Odin's[9] royal throne,
Eye of the world, far blazing Sun !
Wert thou but mine, thy radiant face
As buckler should my Frithiof grace."

"Thou beacon in our Father's home,
Thou Moon, that palely bright dost roam !
Wert thou but mine, thy visage fair
I'd give to grace my maiden there."

But Hilding said, " O foster son,
Set not thy heart her love upon,
For Destiny thy wish gainsaid ;
King Belé's daughter is the maid!

" From Odin's self, in starry sky,
Descends her ancestry so high ;
But thou art Thorsten's son, so yield,
And leave to mightier names the field."

But Frithiof laughed : " My noble race
Counts downward from the death embrace
With which I slew the forest's pride :
I gained his pure blood with his hide.

" A free born man will never yield,
To him belongs the earth's fair field,
And Fate, which oft on him doth frown,
May bear on wings of hope a crown.

" All Might is noble held by Thor[10],
In Thrudvang[11] first the light who saw.
Not birth but worth sits by his board ;
A mighty noble is the sword !

" I'll struggle for my youthful bride,
Were it with Thor the Thunderer's pride.
Be then secure, my lily white,
Who part us dares, must Frithiof fight."

KING BELÉ AND THORSTEN VIKINGSSON.

———•———

ON his sword leant King Belé, and by him stood
The bold Thorsten Vikingsson, his vassal good ;
Scarred like a runic pillar, a hundred years
Had passed o'er the old warrior's silvery hairs.

They stood like two grim temples on a bleak shore,
Ruined, but sacred to the old gods of yore,
With many a line of wisdom writ on their walls,
And many an old-world memory their form recalls.

" Dim evening comes anon," King Belé said ;
" I cannot brook my helmet nor quaff my mead.
Mine eye grows dark, and faintly I draw my breath,
But Valhalla shines nearer.   I hail thee, Death.

" I've called my sons together, and thine also,
That we may e'en take counsel before I go.
I'll give a warning to them, the eagles' young,
Before that death for ever confounds my tongue."

Into the hall together then come the three,
And first 'mongst them came Helgé, dark-visaged he :
He loved to dwell in forests, 'midst altars round,—
With blood upon his fingers he now was found.

Then followed him young Halfdan, with locks so fair,
And features soft and noble, but girlish air ;
And by his side he carried a flimsy blade,
But seemed in warlike trappings a girl arrayed.

But after them came Frithiof, in mantle blue—
He by a head was taller than th' other two.
He stood between the brethren, as day should light
Between the rosy morning and darksome night.

"My children," said the monarch, "my sun goes down.
In union rule the kingdom, and wear the crown ;
For union holds together.   A ring is wrought
Around a lance—without it, its strength is nought.

"Let Force be but a watchman to guard the port ;
Within let concord flourish, with blessings fraught.
The sword was given for safety, and nothing more ;
The shield should be a padlock on the barn door.

" Who his own land oppresses, that foolish man
Can nought but that accomplish his people can.
Upon a barren mountain the forest's pride
Soon withers up, tho' verdant ; its roots are dried.

" Above us rests the heaven on pillars four ;
The throne is founded really upon the law.
Woe to the land and people where force prevails !
But to preserve a kingdom justice ne'er fails.

" Helgé, the gods may tarry in Disarsal ;
But not like to the cockle within its shell.
As long as sunlight glances on meadows wide,
As long as Fancy wanders, the gods abide.

" Entrails are oft deceptive in offered bird,
And oft has proved fallacious the runic word.
The honest heart, O Helgé, and brave beside,
Odin with runes has covered which ne'er deride.

" Perhaps 'tis strange, King Helgé, but still 'tis true :
The sword which bites the sharpest is yielding too.
Mildness adorns the monarch, as flowers the shield,
And spring-time more than winter blesses the field.

" A friendless man is helpless, how strong he be ;
He dies, as in the desert, a barkless tree.
A man by friendship doth like a tree prevail,
Which, watered by a streamlet, defies the gale.

" Count not upon thy father ; struggle alone.
Canst thou not bend the bow, son, 'tis not thine own.
Rest not upon the heroes who buried be ;
Swift streams of their own vigour cleave thro' the sea.

" And though 'tis good, my Halfdan, to laugh and sing,
Gossip becometh no man, far less a king ;
For mead is brewed with hops, son, honey not aye ;
Put steel into your sword, king, earnest in play.

" For too much wit hath no man, e'en 'mongst the wise;
Yet many a man knows something who never tries.
Men scorn the foolish stranger with little wit ;
The wise command attention, though low they sit.

" To find a friend, O Halfdan, a foster-brother,
The way is short, tho' distant from one another.
The castle of a foeman, or his abode,
Should aye be very distant, though on the road.

" Choose not the idle trifler to share your cup—
The empty house stands open, the rich shut up.
Choose one—it is not needful the man to show ;
The world doth know, O Halfdan, what three men know."

Thorsten arose thereafter, and he spoke so :
" The king must not all lonely to Odin go.
We've shared life's toils together, my king and friend,
Together to Valhalla we'll gladly wend.

" Old age and care, son Frithiof, have spoken to me,
Whispering with many a warning I now give thee.
Though godlike Odin's ravens die in the North,
The old man's lips still utter warnings of worth.

" First, give the gods all honour, whate'er betide,
For storm and sunshine hover where they abide.
They see the heart's dark chamber, and judgment make,
And many years scarce expiate the hour's mistake.

" Obey the king'; he governs *alone* my son.
Dark night hath many beacons, the day but one.
A true man ever, Frithiof, abides the best ;
The sword with edge and hilt, son, stands every test.

" Great strength is God's own gift ; but, Frithiof, mind,
That strength, to be true power, must knowledge find.
The bear, by one man conquered, hath twelve men's force ;
The shield doth guard the sword-cut, and stop its course.

" The proud by few are feared, hated of course ;
And haughtiness, O Frithiof, is ruin's source.
Full many a bird soars boldly, but then is struck ;
For storms destroy the harvest, and ill winds luck.

" Praise thou the sun, O Frithiof, when it is sunk,
Good counsel, when 'tis followed, and ale when drunk.
A youth must on his merit for much depend ;
But strife doth prove the falchion, and need the friend.

" Night trust not, nor, in spring-time, the driven snow,
Nor sleeping snake, nor sighing of maiden low ;
Like swiftly-rolling chariot her fancy ranges,
And 'neath her snowy bosom her heart e'er changes.

" Thyself must die, relinquish thy dearest ties ;
But I know one thing, Frithiof, which never dies—
It is the dead man's judgment.   Keep this in sight ;
Therefore choose what is noble, do what is right."

So warned his son that ancient, in that high hall,
As many a scald has sung since in Havamal [2] ;
From race to race the warnings pithy go forth,
And in the deep, dull distance whispers the North.

Then spake they both together words full of worth,
All of their faithful friendship, famed in the North ;
How unto Death still steadfast, in wind and weather,
Their rough old hands in union they'd held together.

" For back to back we've stood, sons, in many a field ;
Wherever fell the death-stroke it met a shield.
Before you now to Valhalla we old ones haste,
And may your fathers' spirit upon you rest."

Much spake the king of Frithiof's heroic mood,
And mighty strength, more goodly than kingly blood.
And much spake aged Thorsten about the glory
Which waits the royal brethren in future story.

" Now hold ye fast together, my children three !
The North three better warriors shall never see ;
For when a powerful monarch doth wisdom wield,
'Tis like the dark steel edging round golden shield.

" Greet ye my daughter also, the rosebud sweet ;
She hath been reared in quiet, as it was meet ;
Protect her,—do not suffer the storm's dark power
To fasten on his helmet this lovely flower.

" My last behest, O Helgé, on thee I lay,—
To love and cherish Ingeborg, from day to day.
Force wounds the noble temper, but kindness leads
Both man and woman, Helgé, to righteous deeds.

" But lay us gently, children, where the blue wave,
Beating harmonious cadence, the shore doth lave ;
Its murmuring song is pleasant unto the soul,
And like a lamentation its ceaseless roll.

" And when the moon's pale lustre around us streams,
And midnight dim grows radiant with silver beams,
There will we sit, O Thorsten, upon our graves,
And talk of bygone battles by the dark waves.

"And now, farewell, my children!　Come here no more;
Our road lies to Allfather's far-distant shore,
E'en as the troubled river sweeps to the sea :
By Frey[3] and Thor and Odin blessed may ye be."

III.

FRITHIOF SUCCEEDS TO HIS FATHER.

LAID in the grave was King Belé and with him Thorsten
    his vassal,
Where they themselves had chosen: by the side of the
    murmuring ocean
Tall tombs lifted their heads; but death their two
    bosoms had parted.
Helgé and Halfdan, by popular choice, now took their
    paternal
Heritage as joint rulers; but only son of his father
Was Frithiof; so took he his castle of Framnäs in quiet.
Three miles broad and long round the castle's dominions
    extended,
Valleys and hills and mountains, but on the fourth
    side the ocean.
Birchwoods crowned the hill-tops, whose smooth slopes
    gently declining,

Gladdened the eye with corn and tall rye gracefully
    waving.
Deep lakes, countless in number, their mirrors held to
    the mountains,
Held to the forests, in whose depths the lofty-plumed
    elm trees
Ruled in their silent domain and drank of the swift-
    rushing torrent.
Scattered within the deep valleys and glades, there
    cropped the green pasture
Herds with glistening skin and udders that longed for
    the milk-pail.
Countless flocks of snowy-fleeced sheep were sprinkled
    amongst them,
Not unlike to the light fleecy clouds which one oft sees
    in spring-time
Cover the blue vault of heaven, when boisterous March
    winds are blowing.
Coursers swift twenty-four, obstreperous whirlwinds
    imprisoned,
Pawing stood in their stalls and pulled at the hay in the
    mangers,
Flowing manes plaited with red and bright hoofs polished
    and iron-shod.
Built of the hardest of timber, the drinking-hall looked
    like a palace.

Not five hundred men (ten times twelve to the
    hundred)
Filled that spacious hall, when assembled to celebrate
    Yuletide.
Made of evergreen oak, down the hall ran a ponderous
    table,
Polished and bright as a breastplate : and there was the
    seat of the chieftain,
At the end; and formed of two gods carved in wood
    were its pillars—
Odin the Lord of the World and Frey with the sun on
    his helmet.
Seated upon his bearskin, Thorsten was lately between
    them
(Coal-black the skin, and scarlet the mouth, with claws
    made of silver)
Amongst his friends, like Hospitality seated 'midst
    Gladness.
Oft, when the moon flew high mid the clouds, the old
    man related
Stories of foreign shores he had seen and of sea-rovers'
    dangers,
Far in the East and the North and the boisterous shores
    of the Baltic.
Still sat the listening warriors and hung on the lips of
    their chieftain,

Like the bee on the rose; but the poet thought upon
   Bragé[1]
With his silvery beard and runes from his lips sweetly
   flowing,
Under the wide-spreading beech, and relating a story by
   Mimer's[2]
Ever-murmuring wave; a history now in himself.
In the midst of the straw-strewn pavement the bright
   glowing hearthstone
Cheerily burnt 'twixt its slabs; and through the atmo-
   sphere murky
With smoke, the stars peeped into the hall, the heavenly
   companions.
Round the walls on nails of steel hung many a helmet,
Burnished and glitt'ring coats of mail, whilst sometimes
   between them
Flashed down a sword like lightning, or like to a meteor
   in winter.
Yet more than helmets and swords with shields the
   hall was resplendent,
Like the disc of the sun or moon, shining with bright
   polished silver.
A maiden went round the table and replenished each
   goblet,
And cast her eyes to the ground; she blushed, and her
   face in the bucklers

Shone back and 'blushed again; this gladdened the
    revelling warriors.

Rich was the house; and wherever the eye was cast the
    spectator

Saw nought but comfort and plenty and storehouses
    crammed unto bursting.

Many a jewel was also concealed, of conquest the
    booty,

Silver and gold resplendent thereon, all skilfully graven.

Yet three things were prized above all these riches in
    value;

The sword handed down from father to son was first of
    the triad,

Angurvadel was its name, of lightning the brother.

Far in the unknown East was it forged (for thus saith
    the story);

In the fires of the dwarfs was it tempered; first worn by
    Björn Blatand.

But Björn lost his life and his sword at once in a battle,

Southwards in Gröningasund, where he fought with
    valorous Vifell.

Vifell a son had called Viking. A king with his
    beauteous daughter

Dwelt at Ulleraker in quiet, but aged and failing.

See, there comes from the depths of the forest a hideous
    giant,

Taller by far than the sons of men, but rough like a wild
  boar,
Demanding the maid and the kingdom to buy his for-
  bearance.
But none dared the combat unequal, nor was there a
  falchion
Could cut through his skull of iron, whence his name
  Jernhos.
Viking alone, just fifteen years old, accepted the chal-
  lenge,
Trusting his strength and relying on Angurvadel.   With
  one sword-cut
Asunder he clove the loud-roaring brute and delivered
  the fair one.
Viking delivered the sword to Thorsten his son, and
  from Thorsten
Came it to Frithiof an heirloom ; when he drew it, its
  shimmer
Flew through the room like lightning or northern
  aurora.
Hilt was of hard-hammered gold ; but the blade was
  engraven
With letters mysterious, unknown in the North, but well
  comprehended
Towards the sun[3], of our fathers the home till the gods
  brought us hither.

Faint and dull looked the runes alway when peace was
    prevailing :
But when Hildur[4] began his sport, then constantly burnt
    they
Red as the comb of the cock when he fighteth ; a lost
    man was he who
In combat encountered that blade with the runes all a-
    flaming.
The sword was famed far and wide, and of swords was
    first in the North.

Next highest in worth was prized a wide-renowned armlet,
Forged by the Vulcan of Northern story, by Vaulund the
    limping ;
Three marks was it in weight and made of the purest of
    fine gold ;
Heaven was designed thereon, with the fortresses of the
    Immortals,
Twelve, like the changing months, but named by the
    poets the sunhouse.
Alfhem too was pourtrayed, the castle of Frey : 'tis the
    sun who[5],
New-born at Christmas, commences to climb the steep
    slopes of heaven.
Söquaback also was there, in whose hall sat Odin with
    Saga[6],

Drank his wine from the golden cup ; but that cup was
    the ocean,

Coloured with gold and the glow of the morning ; and
    Saga was spring-time,

Written on verdant fields ; but instead of the runes were
    the flowers.

Also Balder appeared on his throne, like the sun at mid-
    summer,

From the firmament pouring his riches, of Goodness the
    emblem ;

For Goodness is far-beaming light, but Evil is darkness.

Always to fertilise deigns not the sun, and Beneficence
    likewise

Totters upon the edge of the gulf ; with a heart-rending
    sigh

Vanish they both to the shadows of Hel ; 'tis the story
    of Balder.

Glitnir[7], the city of peace, was seen ; and carefully
    weighing

All things with balance in hand sat Forseti, judge of
    the autumn.

These significant shapes with others, the struggle
    betokening

Of light in heaven's blue vault and the senses of
    mortals,

Were carved by a master's hand. A magnificent cluster

Of rubies its circlet crowned as the sun crowns the
    heavens.

Long in the race was the ring an heirloom, for 'twas
    descended,

Though by the mother's side, from Vanlund, reckoned its
    founder.

Once on a time was the rare jewel stolen by the sea-rover
    Soté,

Who infested the seas of the North, and 'twas not re-
    covered.

Then 'twas whispered that Soté, not far from the bleak
    shores of Bretland,

Living with ship and goods, had buried himself in his
    barrow ;

Yet found he no rest, for the tomb was constantly
    haunted.

Thorsten soon heard of the rumour, and mounted his
    galley with Belé,

Which ploughed through the foaming deep till he came
    to the barrow.

Large as a temple or royal abode, the tomb was em-
    bedded

In ruins and turf-covered banks, which nearly concealed
    it ;

Light also shone therefrom ; through a chink in the
    mouldering portal

Peeped the warriors in : the well-tarred sea-rovers' galley

Stood there with anchor and masts and yards ; but high
 o'er the rudder

Sat a terrible shape ; and 'twas clad in a fiery mantle.

Gloomy and fierce sat it there, and scraped at its blood-
 speckled falchion,

But those drops were not to be cleansed ; all the gold it
 had plundered

Lay scattered around ; and on its arm was hanging the
 armlet.

" Descend we the tomb," whispered Belé, " and hew down
 the demon,

Two 'gainst a spirit of fire !" But Thorsten, half-
 angered, gave answer :

" One against one was our fathers' wont; alone will I
 conquer."

Long argued they now who first of the twain should endeavour

To enter those perilous gates ; till the king seized his
 helmet

And shook two lots therein : now by the glimmering
 starlight

Thorsten beheld his fortune ; then with one blow of his
 iron lance

Burst he the bolts and bars and descended. If one de-
 manded

What he perceived in the noisome pit, he was silent and
    shuddered.

Belé first heard a song, which seemed like the song of a
    demon,

Then a clinking sound, as of blades which on armour are
    clattering,

Then a terrible shriek, then all silent.   Out started
    Thorsten,

Pale, distracted, and shaken, for with Death had he
    struggled.

Yet bore he the ring: " Dearly bought is the prize," said
    he often,

" For I trembled but once in my life, and 'twas when I
    seized it !"

The jewel was famed far and wide, and of jewels was first
    in the North.

Lastly Ellida, the galley, was one of the household
    treasures.

Once on a time when Viking, 'tis said, was returning from
    warfare,

Sailing along the coast he perceived a man on a ship-
    wreck,

Carelessly drifting along as if he derided the breakers.

The man was tall and of noble aspect, and his counte-
    nance open,

Cheerful, yet changeable too, as the sea which sports in
    the sunshine.

His mantle was blue, and his belt of gold, ornamented
    with coral,

Beard white as the foam of the sea, and tresses of sea-
    green.

Viking steered his ship to the spot and succoured the
    suff'rer,

Took him benumbed to his house, and well entertained
    him.

But when invited to rest in his chamber, then laughed he
    and answered :

" Fair is the wind and my ship, as thou seest, is by no
    means a bad one,

A hundred miles, I hope, I shall this night accomplish ;

Thanks for thy courteous reception, 'tis well meant, could
    I only

Leave a remembrance behind ! But my riches lie in the
    ocean.

Yet to-morrow mayst thou find on the shore a
    memento."

By the sea stood Viking next morning, when, lo ! as an
    eagle

Swiftly pursues his prey, into the creek scuds a war-ship.

No form was seen on the deck, and without the aid of a
    helmsman

The rudder steered its course amongst rocks and perilous
    shallows ;

Reefed by themselves were the sails; without the aid of
    a mortal

The anchor dropped of itself, and gripped in the sands of
    the ocean.

Viking stood still and watched, when playfully chanted
    the billows :

" Ægir[8] assisted forgets not his debt, he gives thee the
    war-ship."

A royal gift to behold, for the swelling planks of its frame-
    work

Were not fastened with nails, as is wont, but *grown* in
    together.

Its shape was that of a dragon when swimming, but for-
    ward

Its head rose proudly on high, the throat with yellow gold
    flaming ;

Its belly was spotted with red and yellow, but back by
    the rudder

Coiled out its mighty tail in circles, all scaly with silver;

Black wings with edges of red ; when all were expanded

Ellida raced with the whistling storm, but outstript the
    eagle.

When, filled to the edge with warriors, it sailed o'er the
    waters,

You'd deem it a floating fortress, or warlike abode of a
    monarch.
The ship was famed far and wide, and of ships was first
    in the North.

These and much more received Frithiof as heir to his
    father;
Scarcely was found in the whole of the North an inherit-
    ance fairer,
If 'twere not the son of a king, for a king's worth is
    greatest.
He was not the son of a king, though truly his temper
    was kingly,
Sociable, noble and mild, and each day his glory grew
    greater.
Beside him sat twelve warriors, grey-haired princes of
    exploit,
His father's companions, with breasts of steel and deep-
    scarréd foreheads.
On the warriors' bench, of like age with Frithiof, a young
    man
Sat like a rose among withering leaves : and Björn was
    he named,
Glad as a child, but firm as a man, and wise as an elder.
He had grown up with Frithiof, their blood was mingled
    together,

Foster-brothers in Norland fashion, and bound by agree-
   ment
Together to hold in weal or woe, and by dark oaths of
   vengeance.
Girt round by warriors and guests who had come to the
   funeral banquet,
With eyes full of tears sat Frithiof, a sad entertainer;
Drank, as his fathers were wont, to his father's remem-
   brance and listened
Whilst thundered the skalds to his praise a loud lamen-
   tation;
Then up to his father's seat, now his own, he ascended,
'Twixt Odin and Frey; but Thor's place is up in Val-
   halla.

IV

FRITHIOF'S COURTSHIP.

— ◆ —

In Frithiof's hall loud rings the song,
And poets praise his race so long.
But the song brings
No joy to Frithiof; he hears not what the poet sings.

The earth again in green is drest,
The sea again bears ships on its breast.
But the hero's son
Wanders alone in the woods and looks at the moon.

Lately was he so cheerful and glad,
For gladsome King Halfdan as guest he had,
And Helgé sinister,
And with them they had their lovely sister.

He had sat by·her side and her hand caressed,
And felt in return his own slightly pressed,
　With ardent gaze
He had looked on her noble and lovely face.

And much they talked of the joyful day,
When morning's dew on life still lay.
　The noble mind
With wreaths of roses childhood's hours doth bind.

She hailed him now from each valley and park,
From the name which he cut in the birch's bark,
　And from the wold
Where the sturdy oaks thrive in the heroes' mould.

" It was not so pleasant in the king's ward,
For Halfdan was childish, and Helgé hard.
　The royal brothers
Heard nought but prayers and praise from others.

" And no one " (here blushed she like a rose)
" To whom one might a complaint disclose.
　And in the palace
How confined was it too after Hilding's valleys!

" And the doves which they had tamed and paired
Had flown away, by the fierce hawk scared.
One pair alone
Lingered behind, of these two take thou one.

" The dove he will soon fly home again,
Away from his mate he will not remain ;
Bind under his wing
A friendly line, which unperceived 'twill bring."

Thus whispered they on from morning gray
Till dewy eve the hours away ;
As the evening breeze
In spring-time whispers amongst the rustling trees.

But now she is gone, and Frithiof's joy
Is flown with her.   The unhappy boy
All lonely lies,
And silent thinks of her, and thinks again and sighs.

His sorrow then on a slip he wrote,
And glad let fly the dove with his note ;
But, alas ! hard fate !
The dove came not back, but remained with his mate.

This conduct was not to the mind of Björn,
Who said : " Why doth our eagle mourn ?
Why so sad and oppressed ?
Have his wings been crippled or pierced in his breast ?

" What wilt thou ?   Have we not more than we need
Of yellow pork and dark brown mead ?
Doth not the sound
Of music and song in our halls resound ? "

" The pawing charger stamps in his stall,
For his quarry the falcon screams in the hall.
But Frithiof roves
Alone in the clouds, and thinks of his loves.

" Ellida tosses upon the sea,
And tugs at her anchor constantly.
Ellida, hush !
Frithiof for warlike adventure cares not a rush.

" A death-bed on straw is death ; but I fear
I shall hasten my end at last with my spear.
We cannot fail,
Welcomed guests shall we be to Hela[1] pale ! "

Then Frithiof went his ship aboard,
The white sail swelled and the billows roared.
Right over the bay
To the royal brothers he steered his stormy way.

They were seated on Belé's tomb, and o'er
The common folk administered law.
But Frithiof speaks,
And his voice re-echoes round valleys and peaks.

" Ye kings, my love is Ingborg fair ;
To ask her in marriage I here repair ;
And what I require
I here maintain was King Belé's desire.

" He let us grow in Hilding's care,
Like two young saplings, year by year ;
And therefore, kings,
Unite the full-grown trees with golden rings.

" My father was neither earl nor king,
Yet poets oft his glories sing.
The high-arched grave
Relates the story of my fathers brave.

" Well might I win a kingdom broad,
But keep for my native land my sword.
My shield of proof
Shall guard the royal hall and peasant's roof.

" We are on Belé's tomb : beneath
He lies, attentive to each breath.
With Frithiof prays
The old man in the grave : think well on what he says."

Then rose up Helgé, and said, with scorn :
" Our sister is not for a freeman [2] born.
The kings of the land
May struggle, not thou, for the damsel's hand.

" Boast on, if thou wilt, to be first in the North,
To conquer in war and in love go forth ;
But Odin's blood
I yield not a victim to haughty mood.

" As to my kingdom and throne, I can
Protect it myself.   Wilt be my man ?
A place I proffer
Amongst my house-carls ; wilt take my offer ?"

" Hardly thy man," said Frithiof; " and more,
I am man for myself, as my father before.
From thy scabbard wide
Leap, Angurvadel! thou may'st not abide."

The blue blade glanced in the beaming sun,
And crimson flamed the runes thereon.
Said Frithiof now :
" Of right noble descent, Angurvadel, art thou !

" And had it not been for the tomb where we stand,
I had hewed thee down, dark king, with this hand.
Yet will I show
What my blade can do by a single blow."

So saying, he smote with a mighty stroke
King Helgé's shield, which hung on an oak.
The half-circles twain
Clashed on the tomb, which re-echoed again.

" Well struck, my blade !   Lie still, and pant
For higher deeds ; till then consent
To quench thy fire.
Now sail we home o'er the billow dire."

V.

KING RING.

—◆—

AND King Ring pushed back his chair from the board,
All the warriors about
Rose up to hear the words of their lord,
In the North adored,
He was wise as god Mimer, as Balder devout.

Like the grove was his land where the gods abide,
And war's dark doom
Came not within its shadowy pride ;
And meadows wide
Flourish secure instead, and roses bloom.

Justice, both mild and strict, was set
On the judgment chair ;
And peace discharged each year her debt.
The stranger met
On every side the yellow cornfields there.

And the galleys came with bosom black
And pinions white ;
When from foreign shores they scudded back,
There was no lack
Of wealth with which the rich to delight.

Peace dwelt with freedom as it ought,
In union glad.
And all their chieftain's welfare sought,
Though in the court
Both king and yeoman equal hearing had.

For thirty years peaceful and blessed,
The North he swayed,
And no man injured went to his rest ;
The people blest
His name, and to Odin for him prayed.

And King Ring pushed back his chair from the board,
And every man
Stood up to list to the words of his lord,
In the North adored ;
But he heaved a deep sigh and thus began :

"My queen sits now by Freya there,
With radiant look ;
But here the grass doth flourish fair,
With blossoms rare,
Above her ashes by the brawling brook.

"Ne'er find we a queen so good and fair,
The pride of our lands.
She is gone to breathe Valhalla's air,
But my people's prayer
A queen, a mother demands.

"King Belé, who oft did sail to my hall,
When summer settles,
Did leave a daughter ; my choice doth fall
On the lily small
With rosy morn on its petals.

"I know she is young, and a youthful maid
Would fain pluck flowers;
But withering Winter his hand hath laid
On my whitening head,
And old age above me lowers.

" Can she to my declining head
Affection bring ;
And to my little ones stand in the stead
Of a mother dead,
Then Autumn offers his throne to Spring.

" Take jewels rich from the casket strong
Of every sort ;
Follow, ye skalds, the rest among,
For the god of song
Is present at wooing, and present at sport."

Now out streamed the youths the road along,
With gold and prayers,
And the skalds they followed, a line full long,
With many a song,
And arrived at the hall of King Belé's heirs.

Three wassail nights they kept awake,
But on the fourth
They desired King Helgé answer to make,
That they might take
A quick return to the North.

King Helgé he offered both hawk and horse
In the verdant grove,
And questioned the priests at the oracle's source,
Which were the best course
For his sister, and for her love.

But priests and entrails denied consent
So constantly,
That Helgé, affrighted, his answer sent,
And No it meant;
For when gods ordain must mortals obey.

But gay King Halfdan he laughed and said,
" Farewell to the feast !
King Greybeard must now abandon the maid
But I'll gladly aid
The old man to mount his beast."

Angrily went the envoys away,
And tidings bore
Of the slight to the king; but he drily did say,
That with small delay
King Greybeard will wash out the stain with gore.

He struck his war-shield, which did rest
On a lofty lime :
Straight o'er the brine the galleys pressed
With blood-red crest,
Whilst the nodding plumes to the oars keep time.

A challenge bade Helgé draw the sword,
Who said sinister,
" King Ring is mighty, the strife will be hard,
In Balder's ward,
In his temple I've placed my sister."

There sits the loving heart, full of pain,
And sad her bosom.
She broiders with silk and gold again,
But like the rain
Flow her tears, or the dew on the blossom.

VI

FRITHIOF PLAYS AT CHESS.

———+———

BJÖRN and Frithiof sat and played
At a chessboard fairly made.
Set around with jewels rare,
Of gold and silver was each square.

Then stept Hilding in : "Sit down
In the seat beside mine own,
Drain a goblet, whilst I end
This contest, well-beloved friend ! "

Hilding said : " Of Belé's heir
I bear to thee the rueful prayer.
Ill news hath reached the royal ear,
Hope of thy race, and foeman's fear."

Frithiof said : "O Björn, take heed,
Your king is now hard pressed indeed.
By a pawn he may be freed ;
They are made for kings in need."

"Frithiof, anger not the kings,
Powerful wax the eagles' wings ;
Though 'gainst Ring they weak may seem,
They are strong for thee, I deem."

" Björn, you threaten now the rook,
Thine assault I lightly brook.
'Tis hard, indeed, the rook to o'erpower
When firmly seated in his tower."

" Ingeborg in Balder's shrine
Sits and weeps, and there doth pine.
Can *she* not lure thee to the fight,
Drooping maid with eyes so bright ?"

" Björn, the queen you vainly chase
Was dear to me from childhood's days,
She, the best piece in all the game,
Should sure be saved whatever came.

" Frithiof, wilt thou not decide ?
Must thy foster-father ride
Unheard from thy gates, the whilst
Thou thyself with chess beguil'st ?"——

Then rose Frithiof up and laid
Hilding's hand in his, and said :
" Father, thou hast heard already,
My soul's resolve is firm and steady.

" Let the sons of Belé know
What I've said : I strike no blow
For those who have mine honour slighted,
But I'll see that honour righted."——

" Well, defend thine own fair fame,
I cannot thine anger blame.
Odin guide and bless thee, son ! "
Thus said Hilding, and was gone.

VII

FRITHIOF'S GOOD FORTUNE.

KING BELÉ's sons may gladly roam
From dale to dale, with flag unfurled.
'Tis nought to me; in Balder's dome,
There rests my soul, there lies my world;
There shall no thought my bliss destroy
Of kingly rage or earthly care;
But only drink without alloy
The cup of bliss with Ingborg fair.

Whilst the bright sun with radiance plays,
Sheds on the flower its crimson warm,
Like to the rosy gauze whose haze
Conceals the charms of Ingborg's form;
So long I wander on the strand,
Consumed by everlasting fire,
And, sighing, write upon the sand
Her name, with love that nought can tire.

How slowly pass the lazy hours!
O Delling's son, why tarriest thou?
Hast thou not seen both tombs and towers,
And lakes and islands, until now?
Is there no maid in the far West
To hasten on thy lagging pace;
Who, closely to thy bosom pressed,
Will look into thy radiant face?

At last, in spite of billows' roar,
Thou sink'st into the troubled deep,
And Evening draws her veil before
The mystery of godlike sleep.
Their tale of love the streamlets smother,
The winds their songs of love repress,
Welcome, O Night!   Of gods the mother,
With pearls upon thy bridal dress!

Silent the shining stars advance,
Like lover, tiptoe, to his maid.
O'er the rough wave, Ellida, dance,
Dance on, nor let thy course be stayed.
There, in the distance, lies the grove—
O'er the blue wave, a green line thin—
And Balder's temple is above,
And Love's fair goddess is within.

E 2

O Earth, I could embrace thee now !
O fields, I could thy bosom kiss !
O flowers, which red and white do grow
Upon the rugged precipice !
O Moon, who shed'st thy radiant beams
O'er grove and temple, tomb and tower,
And sit'st like prophetess who dreams
Of things below with silent power !

Who taught thee, brook, the voice which fails,
And dies unspoken in my breast ?
Who taught you, northern nightingales,
To warble forth my love expressed ?
The evening's blushes paint her form
All rosy on the darkening sky ;
But Freya damps its colours warm,
And, envious, sweeps them now away.

Yet gladly let her phantom vanish ;
She comes herself, with bright blue eyes,
And faith, which nought but Death can banish,
She comes herself, affection's prize.
Come, my beloved, let me press thee
To the heart which holds thee dear.
My soul's delight, may Heaven bless thee ;
Come to my arms, and rest thee there.

Slim as the stalk of any flower,
Round as the form of full-blown rose,
With purity thy native dower,
Thy love thou may'st with warmth disclose.
Kiss me, my fair one.   Let the glow
Which warms my veins e'en quicken thee.
Ah ! heaven above and earth below
Swim round me when thou kissest me.

Be not afraid—there is no fear ;
Björn stands below, with sails unfurled,
And warriors armed with shield and spear,
Fit to defend us 'gainst a world.
O that the Fates would so decide
That I might die for thee e'en now,
And joyful to Valhalla ride,
If my Valkyria [1] wert thou.

What whisper you of Balder's ire?
The pious god—he is not wrath.
He loves himself, and doth inspire
Our love—the purest he calls forth.
The god with true and steadfast heart,
The sun upon his glittering form,
Is not his love for Nanna part
Of his own nature, pure and warm ?

There is his image ; he is near.
How mild he looks on me—how kind !
A sacrifice to him I'll bear,
The offer of a loving mind.
Kneel down with me ; no better gift,
No fairer sure for Balder is,
Than two young hearts, whose love doth lift
Above the world almost like his.

More unto heaven than to earth
Belongs my love.   Despise it not ;
For heaven it was that gave it birth,
It longeth for that sacred spot.
On high how pure would be our love !
O might I die by foeman's blade,
And glorious rise to realms above,
Clasped in the arms of my pale maid !

When to the fight the warriors ride
From out the silver portals free,
I should repose thy form beside,
A faithful friend, and gaze on thee.
When Valhall's maids around the board
Hand the large mead-horn, foaming high,
To thee I'd whisper low a word
Of love, and heave a tender sigh.

A hut of branches would I build
On some bright isle in dark blue bay,
'Neath trees with slumbering songsters filled,
The darksome night we'd sleep away.
When Valhall's sun again did burn,
(How pure, how glorious, are his beams),
Unto the gods we would return,
Whilst each of home and quiet dreams.

Thy pallid beauty to enhance,
With stars I'd crown thy golden head ;
In Vingolf's [2] hall with thee I'd dance
Till thy pale cheeks were rosy red.
Then from the dance I thee would bring
To the abode of love and peace.
Bragé the silver-haired to sing
Thy bridal song should never cease.

A songster chirps from yonder brake—
The song is from Valhalla's strand.
How the moon shines upon the lake !
She shineth from Death's shadowy land.
The song and moonlight soft portend
A world of love, devoid of care.
My life and love I'd gladly end
With thee, with thee, my Ingeborg fair.

Weep not, for yet the life-blood streams
In my young veins.   Oh ! weep not so;
For love and youth indulge in dreams
Fantastically here below.
Only thine arms toward me stretch,
With thy blue eyes but look on me,
And easily the dreamer fetch
From heavenly happiness to thee.

" Hush ! 'tis the lark." No, 'tis a dove
Cooing within the wood at rest.
The lark is sleeping by his love,
Secure within his downy nest.
O happy birds ! Can ye not sing
The livelong day as free as air ?
Their life is free, free as the wing
Which bears aloft the happy pair.

" See, the day breaks." No, 'tis the light
Guiding the homeward-veering sail ;
Yet may we speak, as yet the night
Covers us with her darksome veil.
Sleep on, O golden star of day,
Delay to mount the arduous hill ;
For me you may your course delay
Till Ragnarök[3], if so you will.

Alas! 'tis vain to hope for night;
See in the east the reddening streaks.
The morning breeze is fanning light
The roses on my darling's cheeks.
A crowd of feathered songsters twitters,
And soars into the cloudless sky;
Nature awakes, and Ocean glitters,
Whilst shadowy night and lovers fly.

Now rises bright the glorious sphere.
Grant me, O golden sun, this prayer,
I know it well—the god is near,
And casts around his dazzling glare.
O thou, who tread'st thine annual course,
Proudly magnificent as now,
And cloth'st in light from glory's source
Victorious thy sacred brow,

I place before thy glitt'ring eye
The fairest thing within the North;
Take her into thy ward, most high,
She is thine image upon earth.
Her soul is pure as thy bright beams,
Her eyes are as the heaven blue;
The gold which from thy forehead streams
Reflects in her long tresses' hue.

Farewell, beloved one ; and now
We part until a longer meeting.
Farewell !   A kiss upon thy brow,
Now on thy lips a lover's greeting.
Sleep now, and dream of me ; when soft
You wake at noon, let mem'ry dwell
Upon thy absent love, who oft
Doth sigh and dream of thee.   Farewell !

VIII.

THE FAREWELL.

INGEBORG.

Bright breaks the day, but Frithiof cometh not!
Though yesterday was held in state the court
Upon my father's tomb. Well was the spot selected!
Well may his daughter's fate be there decided.
How many soft entreaties has it cost me,
How many tears, well marked I trust by Freya,
To melt the ice of hate round Frithiof's heart,
And charm the promise from his haughty lips,
Again to ask my hand from my proud brother!
Alas! how hard man is, who for his honour
(So christens he his pride) recketh but little,
O rather, nought at all, if he should torture
A woman's faithful bosom more or less.
Poor woman, closely bounden to his breast,
Is like the lichen blooming on the rock,

With pallid colour, whilst with pain she keeps
Her timid hold upon his stony breast :
And her sole nourishment the tears of night.—
So there my fate was yesterday decided,
And the red sun hath sunk to rest thereon.
But Frithiof cometh not ! The pallid stars
In quick succession quench their fires and vanish ;
And as each planet pales and dies away,
So disappears each hope within my breast.
Yet wherefore did I hope ? Valhalla's gods
Protect me not : I have offended them.
The mighty Balder, in whose shrine I dwell,
Doth frown on me, and sure a human passion
Is all unsanctified in godlike eyes ;
And earthly gladness should not dare to show
Its laughing face beneath the mighty vault
Where the imperial powers of heaven reside.
What is my fault ? Why doth the pious god
Frown darkly on a youthful maid's affection?
Is it not pure as Urda's shining wave[1],
As innocent as Gefjon's[2] morning visions?
The mighty sun turns not away his eye,
Though pure and holy, from two faithful lovers,
And Day's fair widow, star-bespangled night,
Immersed in grief, with joy receives their oaths.
That which is lawful under heaven's blue vault,

Can it be guilty in this sanctuary?
Frithiof I love. Alas! as long ago
As memory stretches backwards have I loved him;
The passion is coeval with my birth,
I know not whence it came, cannot conceive
The thought that it were severed from my being.
Even as the golden fruit its form arranges
Around its kernel in the summer sun,
So have I grown and ripened, and my being
Is but the outer shell of inward love.
Forgive me, Balder! With a faithful heart
I tread thy threshold, and with heart as faithful
Will I depart therefrom; I'll take it with me
Thence over Bifrost's[3] bridge, and place myself
In all my love before Valhalla's gods.
There shall it stand, an Asa[4] son like them,
Mirror itself in shields, and fly away
With soft and dovelike wings right through the blue
And boundless space into Allfather's breast,
From whence it came. Wherefore knittest thou
Thy brows immortal in the morning grey?
Within my veins flows pure as in thine own
The blood of Odin old. What wilt thou, kinsman?
Devoted love I cannot offer thee,
Will not; but still 'tis worthy of thy heaven.
But I can offer thee my life and love,

Cast them away, e'en as a queen doth cast
Her mantle from her, and as heretofore
She is the same, a queen.   It is resolved!
Valhalla's glorious host shall not disown
Their daughter; I will meet my destiny
As many a hero hath!   But here comes Frithiof!
How wild he looks, how pale!   'Tis o'er! 'tis o'er!
My angry Norna[5] stalks beside his form.
Be firm, my soul!   Welcome, though late indeed!
Our destiny is fixed, for I can read
The sentence on thy brow.

FRITHIOF.

Glows it not there
Stamped deep in burning letters, speaking fierce
Of hate and exile?

INGEBORG.

Frithiof, calm thyself,
Relate what has befallen. I have divined
The worst long since ; I am prepared for all.

FRITHIOF.

I reached the court, upon thy father's tomb,
And round its verdant sides, shield touching shield,
Stood sword in hand the warriors of the North,

Crowded in many a dense-packed serried rank
Up to the top; upon the judgment stone,
Black as a thunder cloud, stood cruel Helgé,
The pallid butcher with the evil eye;
And by his side, a fair and stalwart child,
Sat Halfdan, careless playing with his sword.
Then I arose and said : " War is abroad,
And strikes his echoing shield within our borders,
Thy crown and land, King Helgé, are in danger ;
Give me thy sister's hand, and I will use
Henceforth my warlike force in thy defence.
Let then the wrath between us be forgotten,
Unwillingly I strive 'gainst Ingborg's brother.
Secure, O king, by one fraternal act
Thy golden crown and save thy sister's heart.
Here is my hand.   By Thor, I ne'er again
Present it here for reconciliation."
A joyful sound arose.   A thousand swords
Hammered applause upon a thousand shields.
The clash of arms rose to the sky, which glad
Re-echoed its approval, thundering loud :
" Let Ingeborg be his, the slender lily,
The fairest flower which blooms within our vales :
His is the boldest blade within our land,
Let Ingeborg be his !"   Our foster-father,
The aged Hilding, with the silver beard,

Arose and spoke with words of wisdom full,
And many a proverb, trenchant as a blade;
Halfdan himself, from off the royal seat,
Arose, entreating both with look and word.
It was in vain, for every prayer was wasted,
Just as the sunbeam falls upon a rock
And charms no verdure from its barren breast.
Thus was King Helgé's face; a pallid No
To damp the hopes and prayers of mortal men.
"Upon a simple knight," said he with scorn,
"I might bestow my sister; but a profaner
Of temples mates not well with Valhall's daughter.
Hast thou not, Frithiof, broken Balder's peace?
Hast thou not seen my sister in his temple,
When darksome night concealed your secret meeting?
Say yes or no!"   Then rose a mighty shout
Up from the crowd: "Say No, say only No,
We trust thee on thy word, we answer for thee,
Thou Thorsten's son, as good as royal blood;
Say No, say No, and Ingeborg is thine."
"My weal or woe depends upon a word,"
Said I, "be not alarmed for that, King Helgé;
I would not lie myself to Valhall's bliss,
Nor more to earthly.   I have seen thy sister,
Have talked with her by night without the temple;
But Balder's peace have I not therefore broken."

They let me say no more. A cry of horror
Rose from the'crowd; those standing near my side
Shrank back aghast, as from a pestilence;
And when I gazed around, blank superstition
Had lamed each tongue, and painted chalky white
Each cheek but lately burning bright with hope.
King Helgé had succeeded; with a voice
As hoarse and fierce as when the Vala[6] dead,
In Vegtamsquida sang a lay to Odin
Of ruin to the gods and Hel's success,
So hoarse he spoke: "Exile or instant death
I could impose, as by our fathers' laws,
For this thy crime; but I will be as mild
As Balder is, whose temple thou hast outraged;
Far in the west there lies a group of islands
Ruled by Earl Angantyr.
As long as Belé lived the earl presented
Each year his tribute; since he has neglected.
Sail o'er the billow wild and bring the treasure;
I ask this expiation for thy madness."
This said, continued he, with hateful scorn,
"That Angantyr is miserly and loves his gold,
Like to the dragon Fafner; but who indeed
Can brave our modern Sigurd Fafnersbane.
Till the next summer we await thee here,
Bringing thy glory, and 'fore all, the treasure.

F

If not, Frithiof, each man shall call thee niding';
Friendless and homeless shalt thou roam the land.".
He gave his judgment and dismissed the court.

INGEBORG.

And thy resolve?

FRITHIOF.

      Have I a choice to make?
Is not mine honour bound by his demand?
I shall accomplish it if Angantyr
Concealed his gold in Slidur's[8] miry flood.
To-day I must depart.

INGEBORG.

      And leave me here?

FRITHIOF.

Not leave thee, Ingborg; thou wilt follow me.

INGEBORG.

Impossible!

FRITHIOF.

      Hear me before you answer!
Thy cunning brother Helgé hath forgotten

That Angantyr was friendly with my father,
Even as with Belé; it may come to pass
That he will freely give what I demand,
If not, a powerful advocate and sharp
Hangs here.   The precious gold I'll send to Helgé,
And thereby shall we both for ever 'scape
The crowned impostor's bloody arts and crimes.
But we ourselves, fair Ingeborg, will hoist
Ellida's sail and skim the unknown deep;
She'll waft us gently to some friendly shore,
Which will give shelter to our outlawed love.
What care I for the North, what for a people
Which pales with abject fear before their gods,
And with audacious hand assails my heart,
Lays hands upon my sanctuary of love?
By Freya fair, their base designs shall fail!
A wretched thrall is bounden to the soil
Which gave him birth; but I, I will be free,
Free as the mountain breeze.   A clod of earth
From off my father's tomb, and one from Belé's,
Can well be placed on board, and that is all
That we demand from this our fatherland.
Belovèd maiden, there are other suns
Than this which palely lights our snowy fells;
There is a heaven brighter far than this,
Where tranquil stars look down with yellow radiance,

In the warm summer nights, upon the deep
And fragrant laurel groves.
My father, Thorsten Vikingsson, had journeyed
In warlike emprize far and wide and oft,
At eve, when the fire shed its ruddy light,
Discoursed of Greece and of her sunny isles,
Her dark green groves amid the foaming waves.
A mighty race dwelt there in ancient times,
And mighty gods within those marble shrines.
Now are they waste and broken, the grass grows .
On the deserted paths, whilst perhaps a flower
Peeps from the hallowed tomb of former wisdom.
The tall and graceful column oft is seen
Encircled by the verdure of the south,
And there the earth produces without stint
An unsown harvest, all that man requires,
And golden apples blush between the leaves,
And purple grapes hang heavy from the vines,
And swell luxuriant as thine own sweet lips.
There, Ingeborg, we'll form amid the waves
Another north, more beautiful than here;
And with our fond affection we will fill
The graceful temple arches, and delight
With earthly happiness the vanished gods.
When the chance sailor, slowly gliding by,
With flapping sail unruffled by the storm,

Beholds our habitation on the isle,
When evening spreads its crimson light abroad,
He'll gaze and see upon the temple's threshold
The modern Freya (Aphrodité called
In their soft tongue, I trow), and fixed admire
The golden tresses streaming in the wind,
And eyes more bright than are the southern skies.
And afterwards there shall arise around
A little troop of fairies for the temple,
With cheeks where you would deem the sunny south
Her roses with the northern snows had blended.
Ah, Ingeborg, how easily attained
Is earthly joy by two young faithful hearts!
Have they the courage but to seize her fast,
She follows willingly and builds for them.
Another Vingolf here below the clouds.
Come, haste! each idle word we utter here,
Subtracts a moment from our future bliss.
All is prepared; already Ellida
Hath spread her swarthy eagle wings for flight.
The freshening breeze will waft us swift away
For ever from this superstitious shore.
Why hesitate?

INGEBORG.

I cannot follow thee.

FRITHIOF.

Not follow me?

INGEBORG.

Ah! Frithiof, you are happy;
You follow none, and like the mast which stands
Erect upon your galley you go forth,
And steer your course e'en as the rudder doth
Which guides the ship over the boist'rous wave.
How differently placed am I!
My lot is cast by other hands than mine,
Remorselessly they grasp their bleeding prey
To sacrifice herself and weep and grieve
In silence, is the royal maiden's doom.

FRITHIOF.

Art thou not free already? In the tomb
Thy father sits.

INGEBORG.

But Helgé is my father,
Stands in my father's place, on his consent
Depends my hand, and Belé's daughter steals not
Her earthly happiness, how near it be.
What were a woman if she rent asunder
The ties with which the Almighty hath attached

Her slender form to the stern breast of man?
Is she not like the pallid water-lily,
Which rises with the wave and falls again?
The sharp keel passes o'er her prostrate form,
Careless, may be, how sore her breast is wounded.
Such then is woman's fate; but whilst the plant
Holds firm its root within the shifting sand,
It has its beauties, and reflects the light
Sent down from heaven by the pale bright stars,
On the blue deep itself a beauteous star;
But breaking from its root it drifts away,
A withered leaf upon the watery waste.
Last night, a long long weary night to me,
I waited for thee and thou camest not;
The children of the night, dark brooding thoughts,
With swarthy locks passed rapidly before
My wakeful eye, tearless and hot with care;
Balder himself, the unstained god, looked down
With glances full of wrath and menace on me.
Last night I have considered well my fate,
And my resolve is taken, I remain
A sacrifice upon my brother's altar.
Well was it for me that I listened not,
When thine imagination conjured up
The lovely isles where the sun never sets
Upon a flowery world of love and peace.

Who knows how weak one is? My childhood's dreams,
Sweet mem'ries now long silenced rise again,
And whisper in mine ear familiar tones,
Dear as a sister's, tender as a lover's.
I listen not; nay, nay, I hear ye not,
Belovèd voices of my childhood's days!
Child of the north, what do I in the south?
I am too pale for its red blushing roses,
My temper is too moderate for its glow;
I should be scorched by its bright blazing sun,
And full of longing I should cast my eyes
Back to the northern star, who constant keeps
A heavenly watch upon our fathers' graves.
My noble Frithiof shall not flee away
From the dear land which proudly owns his birth,
Nor shall he cast away his glory for
A thing so worthless as a maiden's love.
A life in which the sun doth rise and set
On each successive day just like the last,
Always monotonous, is good, perhaps,
For womankind, but for the hero's soul,
And well for thine, a life of calm is ill.
Thy place is where the restless steeds of ocean
Rush madly on the broad and troubled deep;
When on thy deck, amid the clash of arms,
Thou spurnest death and danger for thine honour!

The lovely isle you painted thus would be
The grave of glories yet not thought upon.
And with thy rusted shield would rust likewise
Thy noble temper.   So it shall not be!
I will not steal away my Frithiof's name
From songs of future bards, nor will I quench
My hero's glory in its rosy dawn.
Be wise, my Frithiof, let us bend before
The mighty Nornas ; let us save from off
The shipwreck of our love at least our honour ;
Our fond affection cannot now be saved.
We must part.

FRITHIOF.

        But wherefore must we part ?
Because a sleepless night hath loosed thy nerves ?

INGEBORG.

To save mine honour and thine own from ruin.

FRITHIOF.

On man's affection resteth woman's honour.

INGEBORG.

· He loves not long who loves without esteem.

FRITHIOF.

By light caprice esteem is never gained.

INGEBORG.

The sense of right is sure a noble feeling.

FRITHIOF.

But yesterday our love was not against it.

INGEBORG.

Nor more to-day, but only 'gainst our flight,

FRITHIOF.

Pressing necessity compels us, come!

INGEBORG.

Necessity is what is right and noble.

FRITHIOF.

High rides the sun and fast the time speeds past.

INGEBORG.

Alas! alas! 'tis past, 'tis past for ever!

FRITHIOF.

Consider well; is this thy last resolve?

INGEBORG.

I have considered all, it is my last.

FRITHIOF.

Maiden, farewell! Farewell, King Helgé's sister!

INGEBORG.

O Frithiof, Frithiof, must we thus be parted?
Hast thou no friendly glance to give to me,
The friend of childish days? no hand to reach
To the unfortunate you loved before?
Think you I stand on roses here and watch
With smiling face my happiness depart?
That without pain I tear from out my breast
A hope that grew entwined around my being?
Wert thou not aye my bosom's morning dream?
All joy I had or knew on earth was Frithiof,
And all that life displayed of great or noble
Assumed thy shape before my loving eyes.
Darken not the dear image; do not meet
With cruelty the weak one, when she offers
All that affection prizes on the earth,
All that could make Valhalla's mansions dear.
Frithiof, the sacrifice is hard enough,
A word of comfort might it well deserve.
I know thou lovest me, have known it since

My youthful days began on earth to dawn,
And rest assured thine Ingeborg's remembrance
Follows thee many a year, where'er thou roam'st.
But war's loud clangour drowns the voice of care,
'Tis swept away upon the rolling wave,
And dares not sit upon the warrior's bench,
When the deep mead horn celebrates the victor.
But now and then, when in the quiet night
Before thine eye flit glimpses of the past,
You will distinguish then a pallid form ;
Then scan her visage well, for she salutes you
From regions well belov'd, for 'tis the image
Of the pale girl who dwells in Balder's shrine.
Then turn her not away, albeit her form
Is bent with care, but whisper in her ear
Gently a word of comfort; night's dark wings,
The faithful night, will waft those words to me ;
One comfort left, for other have I none !
There's nought for me which may distract my thoughts;
All that's around me tells me of my loss.
The mighty pile above me speaks alone
Of thee ; the god-like images assume,
When the moon palely shines, thy form and features.
Upon the sea I gaze, there swam thy bark,
And clove the foaming wave to love and me.
I wander in the grove and there I see

My name cut deep in many a forest stem ;
The bark now swells and grows, my name departs,
And that betokens death, so say the seers.
I ask the sun where last he saw thy face,
I ask the night, but still and silent they,
Then the dark sea which bore thee forth, and he
Answers with a deep sigh upon the shore.
When the red sun sinks in the western wave,
A greeting will I send on his bright beams,
And heaven's wayfarers, the travelling clouds,
Shall bear a deep drawn sigh from me to thee.
Thus will I sit within my maiden bower,
After life's joy, a widow clothed in black,
And on the canvas broider broken lilies,
Till one day spring shall weave his web and plant
The earth with better lilies on my grave ;
And when I take the harp, in broken tones
To sing the unceasing grief within thy breast,
My voice will choke with tears—as now.——

FRITHIOF.

Thou conqu'rest, Belé's daughter, weep no more !
Forgive my anger, which was but my sorrow,
Which for the moment took the garb of wrath,
Of wrath, which cannot long 'gainst thee be nurst.
Thou art my guardian angel, Ingeborg ;

The noble mind best teaches what is noble;
The wisdom of necessity could have
No better advocate than thou art now,
Thou shining Vala[9] with the rosy lips.
Yes, I will bend before necessity,
Will part from thee, but not relinquish hope;
I bear it with me o'er the western wave,
I'll bear it with me unto death's dark door.
The coming spring will see me here again,
King Helgé yet again must brook my presence.
When I've performed the task which he demands,
Atoned the crime of which I am accused,
Then will I ask thy hand, nay, will demand it,
In open court, 'mid helms and bristling spears,
Not from thy brother, but from the northern folk,
They are thy lawful sponsors, royal maiden.
I'll have a word with him that says me nay.
Farewell till then, be true, forget me not,
And take in mem'ry of our childhood's love
My armlet here, the work of skilful Vaulund,
With heaven's wonders deep engraved in gold:
The most to be admired a faithful heart.
How gracefully it suits thy snowy arm:
Like glowworm round the tender lily's stem!
Farewell, my love, my bride, again farewell,
Ere many moons have shone all will be well!

                              (*Goes.*)

INGEBORG.

How glad, defiant, and how full of hope!
He plants the glitt'ring point of his good sword
Before the Norna's breast and cries: Submit!
Poor Frithiof, know'st thou not the Norna yields not?
She goes her way and laughs at Angurvadel.
Little thou know'st the temper of my brother!
Thine own heroic mind cannot conceive
The darksome depths of his, and all the hate
Which gnaws and burns within his envious breast.
On thee his sister's hand he'll ne'er bestow;
He'd rather sacrifice his crown and life,
Or offer me to ancient Odin up,
Or to old Ring, whom now he wars against.
Where'er I turn I see no hope for me,
Yet I rejoice it lives within thy breast.
Alone I'll stanch the wound which pierced my heart;
But thee may angels follow and preserve!
Here on thine armlet let me count the days,
Each separate month of long enduring care;
Two, four, or six—and then thou may'st return.
Alas! no more thou'lt find thine Ingeborg!

IX

INGEBORG'S LAMENT.

—◆—

'Tis Autumn now,
Stormily heaveth the sea his brow,
Ah ! but how gladly I'd lie
'Neath the bare sky !

As in a trance,
Watched I his sail o'er the western wave dance.
Ah ! happy sail, thou wilt follow
Frithiof to-morrow.

Blue rolling wave,
Swell not so high o'er the track of the brave.
Shine, ye stars, brightly, and say
Where lies the way.

When it is spring,
He will come home like a bird on the wing;
Vainly he'll search for his maid
In the green glade;

Deep in the mould,
All for her love she lies stiffened and cold,
Or sacrificed perhaps to another
By her dark brother.

Hawk, which he left,
Dearly I'll love thee, of master bereft,
Teach thee to come at my word,
Swift darting bird.

Here on his hand,
Worked on the canvas thou proudly shalt stand,
Silver thy wings, and behold!
Claws made of gold.

Once on a time,
Freya took hawk's wing, and wandered each clime :
North and south the fair rover
Sought for her lover.

If I could borrow
Thy wings, they'd carry me not from my sorrow.
Death is the angel who brings
Godlike wings.

Hawk, come to me,
Sit on my shoulder, and gaze at the sea.
Ah! how we gaze from the spot,
Frithiof comes not.

When I am gone,
He'll come to my grave in silence to mourn ;
Greet then, O greet from Ingborg departed
My love brokenhearted !

X.

FRITHIOF ON THE SEA.

On the stormy strand,
Helgé king did stand
In his fiercest mood,
And called the goblin brood.

See the rainbow dim and dusky,
Thunder rattles round the skies,
And the gale sounds hoarse and husky,
White with foam the ocean lies.
Lightning through the inky clouds
Sudden cuts a blood-red streak,
All the feathered tribes in crowds,
Seek the land with piercing shriek.

" Hard the weather, brothers !
Stormy wings I hear

Fluttering in the distance,
But we tremble not.
Quiet in thy grove
Sit and think of me,
Lovely in thy tears,
Lovely Ingeborg!"

'Gainst Ellida's stem
Came two goblins arrayed ;
'Twas icy cold Ham
And snowy Hejd.

Now are loosed the tempest's wings,
Now the madman dips them deep
In the ocean, now he swings
Then whirling 'gainst heaven's sacred keep.
All the powers of darkness roll,
Riding grim upon the waves,
Up from ocean's foaming bowl,
From his deep, unfathomed caves.

"The journey was fairer,
In the bright moonshine,
O'er the blue breakers
To Balder's shrine.

'Twas warmer than here
'Gainst Ingeborg's heart,
And whiter than sea-foam
Her swelling bosom."

Solundarö we see,
Rise from the wave so white,
There we at rest shall be,
Steer for the haven tight.

But our daring vikings shudder,
Not so soon on sturdy oak,
Joyfully he grasps the rudder,
Spurns away the tempest's stroke.
Higher yet the sail he heaves,
Faster yet the wave he cleaves,
Straight to the west, straight to the west,
We drift upon the billows' breast!

" Gladly I will fight
Yet an hour against the storm,
Storm and Northmen flourish
Together on the brine.
My Ingeborg would blush,
If her eagle of the sea,

Fled afraid, with drooping wings,
In haste unto the land."

Now the waves do roar,
Back the ship doth reel,
The tackle creaketh sore,
And straineth hard the keel.

Yet though wild the wave may thunder,
Rolling darkly far and wide,
Ellida cleaves its rage asunder,
Stout and sturdy is her side.
As a meteor doth shoot,
So darts she by like arrow bright,
She springs like stag or nimble goat,
Lightly by from height to height.

" Better 'twas to kiss
My bride in Balder's shrine,
Than stand here and smack
The salt sea bubbling brine.
I'd rather cast my arms
Around fair Ingeborg's form,
Than stand fast here and grip
This rudder in my hands."

From heaven's lofty fields,
Black with angry frown,
Down on deck and down on shields,
The hailstorm clatters down.

Now between the lofty masts
Nought is seen but darksome night,
Dark as when the trumpet blasts
Shall call the dreaming dead to light.
Storm, by powers of darkness raised,
Will swallow up the reckless brave,
Who, by relentless furies seized,
Will sink into a watery grave.

  " Blue beds in the deep
  Ran prepares for us,
  But I wait for thine,
  Lovely Ingeborg.
  Oars, with powerful stroke
  Urge on Ellida,
  Keel, divinely built,
  Support us yet an hour!"

O'er the starboard lept,
A sea with sudden flush,

The deck was cleanly swept
By the mighty rush.

Frithiof from his arm then takes
Of purest gold a heavy ring,
Bright as sun when up he breaks,
'Twas a gift of Belé king.
In portions then the ring he splits,
Forged by dwarfs with cunning rare,
Parts them 'mongst his crew, omits
None of those who then stood there.

" 'Tis good to have gold
On our last emprise,
No one may descend
To Ran empty handed.
Cold is she to kiss,
Fickle her embrace,
But dearly she loves
The red red gold."

———

With redoubled rage
The storm now thunders on,
Nought can it assuage,
The sheets and yards are gone.

FRITHIOF ON THE SEA.

Now the waves roll onward sailing,
Breaking o'er the vessel rough,
And the crew though always baling,
Cannot yet bale out enough.
Frithiof e'en cannot conceal
Death stalks fearful now on board,
Higher than the gale doth peal,
Or crashing wave, his mighty word.

    " Björn, come hold the rudder,
    Grasp it with thy bearlike arm,
    Valhalla's gods sure never
    Send such storms as these.
    There's witchcraft in the matter,
    Helgé coward summoned
    The spirits from the deep,
    I will up and see ! "

Up the mast he sprang
With a mighty bound,
Like wild cat there did hang
And cast his eyes around.

See, before Ellida's storms
Like a drifting isle, a whale,

And two hideous goblin forms
Ride upon it 'mid the gale.
Hejd, with coat all snowy white,
Like unto a polar bear,
And Ham his wings prepared for flight,
Like eagle stretches in the air.

"Now, Ellida, show me
Whether you possess
Courage in thine iron-bound
Swelling breast of oak.
Listen to my voice,
Thou daughter of the gods,
With thy head of iron,
Gore the magic whale!"

And Ellida heard
Her master's wish,
And sprang at his word
'Gainst the mighty fish.

And a bloody fountain spirts
From the wound towards the sky,
Whilst the monster mad with hurts
Roaring downward quick doth fly.

Then at once two lances part,
By heroic vigour flung,
Pierce the shaggy icebear's heart,
Through the eagle's bosom swung.

    " Ellida, well struck !
    Not so quickly I trow,
    Will King Helgé's warship
    Arise from the deep.
    Hejd and Ham too no longer,
    Will keep the sea, I ween,
    Bitterly bites
    The bright blue steel."——

Now the storm has flown,
The sea is calm awhile,
A gentle swell is blown
Against the neighbouring isle.

Then at once the sun arose,
Like a king who mounts his throne,
Vivifies the world and throws
His light on billow, field and stone.
His newborn beams adorn awhile
A dark green grove on rocky top,

All recognise a sea-girt isle,
Amongst the distant Orkney's group.

"The prayers of Ingeborg
Ascended unto heaven,
Her knees so lily white
Were bent to God in prayer.
Blue eyes filled with tears,
Sighs from swandown bosom,
Have touched the Asa's hearts,
Let us give them thanks!"——

But Ellida's frame,
From the shock of the whale,
Is tired and lame,
And her strength doth fail.

Tired indeed are all on board,
All the crew of Frithiof's men,
Scarce supported by a sword,
Can they raise themselves again.
Björn takes four of them ashore,
On his mighty shoulders wide,
Frithiof singly takes twice four,
Places them the fire beside.

" Blush not, ye pale ones,
The sea's a valiant viking,
'Tis hard indeed to fight ·
Against the rough sea waves.
Lo! there comes the mead horn
On golden feet descending,
To warm our frozen limbs,
Hail to Ingeborg ! "——

XI

FRITHIOF VISITS ANGANTYR.

— · —

WITH all his men, we say,
Angantyr did recline,
And drank so blithe and gay
All in his house of pine,
He was so glad at heart,
The sea he gazed upon,
'Neath which the sun did dart
Just like a golden swan.

Whilst by the window stood
Old Halvar, and took heed,
He watched in serious mood,
With eye upon his mead,
For 'twas the old man's whim
To make a single draught,
Each horn he found near him
Was to the bottom quaffed.

Now shouted he full loud
Into the hall and said ;
" Ship see I on the flood,
Her voyage was not glad,
Death holds her crew as prey,
Now make they for the land,
And two tall giants lay
The pale ones on the strand."——.

Straight o'er the rugged crag
The earl did gaze down too :
" That is Ellida's flag,
With Frithiof 'mongst her crew.
By gesture and by feature
Old Thorsten's son is known,
Within the North no creature
Like majesty doth own."

Then from the festive board
Sprang Atlé up anon,
Black bearded berserk hard,
And fierce to look upon.
He cried : " Now will I shame
The lie that rumour spread,
That Frithiof's sword can tame,
But n'er from foe hath fled."

And up beside him sprang
His twelve companions near,
The earth resounding rang,
And rattled sword and spear.
They streamed down to the strand
Where tired the warriors lay,
And Frithiof on the sand
Encouraged temper gay.

" I easily could slay thee,"
Did Atlé viking cry,
" Yet if thy heart betray thee,
I grant thee leave to fly.
Only for mercy plead,
Although a warrior bold,
And I myself will lead
Thee to the earl's stronghold."

" Though scarce from death restored,"
Replied bold Frithiof wrath,
"'I scarce shall yield my sword
Before I prove its worth."
The mighty blade was swung
Above the warrior's head,
On Angurvadel's tongue
The runes were glowing red.

Now swordcuts fast they ply,
And rattling deathstrokes thunder,
But both their bucklers fly
At the first stroke asunder.
The champions ne'er did quit,
Nor from the circle broke,
Sharp Angurvadel bit
And Atlé's falchion broke.

" Against a swordless man
I scorn to wield my steel,"
Said Frithiof, " but again
We'll try our warlike zeal."
As Autumn breakers shatter
Themselves upon the shore,
So with a deaf'ning clatter
They 'gainst each other bore.

As angry eagles fight
Upon the stormy main,
As bears exert their might,
So wrestle they and strain.
Full many a rock would tumble
Receiving such dire hugs,
The forest oak would humble
His crest before such tugs.

H

On each the sweat stands thick,
And cold each bosom heaves,
Bushes and stones they kick
About like withered leaves.
The steelclad men abide
The end upon the strand,
The contest far and wide
Was famed in Northern land.

At last bold Frithiof sent
His enemy to earth,
Knee on his bosom bent
And spake with words of wrath :
" Had I but my good sword,
Black Berserk beard, I pledge
To thee mine honest word,
That thou should'st feel its edge."

" Be not for that afraid "
Said Atlé without flinch,
" Depart and fetch thy blade,
I will not budge an inch.
At one time or another
We must Valhalla see,
First one and then another,
It soon your turn may be."

With patience long not gifted,
Frithiof the foe would kill,
And Angurvadel lifted,
But Atlé yet lay still.
This touched the hero's soul,
He stayed the sweeping brand
Before it reached its goal,
And took the fall'n one's hand.

Now Halvar cried with zeal,
And raised his snow white wand :
" In this no joy we feel
Put up the murderous brand.
The silver dishes steam
Long since with viands choice,
They now are cold, I deem,
And thirst chokes up my voice."

Now reconciled they be,
Pass through the castle door,
Frithiof had much to see
He never saw before.
To keep out wind and weather,
No coarse wood walls were there,
But costly gilded leather
Adorned with flowers fair.

Upon the pavement glows
The fire with ruddy glare,
But 'gainst the wall arose
Chimney of marble fair ;
No soot the rafters clad,
No smoke above them soars,
And glass the windows had,
Secured with locks the doors.

On silver brackets fair,
The tapers bright are placed,
No torches crackling there
Disturb the warriors' feast.
Now roasted whole they bring
Upon the board a deer,
With hoof in act to spring.
And garlands 'neath each ear.

Behind each chair a maid
Stood with her skin so white,
Bright as a star displayed
Amid a stormy night.
Their nut-brown locks are streaming
Luxuriant from each head,
Their bright blue eyes are beaming,
Their rosy lips are red.

High on a silver throne,
The earl sat in his might,
His helm like sunshine shone,
His mail with gold bedight.
With golden stars designed
His mantle was, and there
Were purple borders lined
With ermine spotless fair.

Then rose he from the board,
Stept forward paces three,
And said with friendly word :
" Come here and sit by me.
Full many a horn I've swallowed
With Thorsten Vikingsson,
The son his path has followed,
And glorious deeds hath done."

Then was the beaker flowing
With wine from Sicily,
Like flaming crimson glowing
And foaming like the sea.
" Welcome my noble guest,
Son of mine ancient friend,
We'll drink to Thorsten blest
Remembrance without end."

A skald from Scotland's hills
Now touches sweet the strings,
Melodious tones distils,
And heroes' exploits sings;
But in the old Norsk tongue,
E'en as our fathers spake,
He Thorsten's deeds then sung,
And no man silence brake.

Now much the earl did speak
Of friends he'd left behind ;
Frithiof did answer make
With mirth and wit combined.
And no man could complain
Of aught he there did tell,
Like Saga² spoke he plain
By Mimer's³ holy well.

And when he did relate
What on the deep he saw,
Of Helgé's monsters' fate,
And goblins triumphed o'er,
Then laughed the warriors all,
And Angantyr he smiled,
And all within the hall
Applauded Fortune's child.

But when he came to speak
Of Ingeborg at last,
How down her gentle cheek
The tears did flow so fast,
Then many a maid did sigh,
Cheeks blushing did attest
How gladly would she fly
Unto her lover's breast !

Patient the earl had heard
The young man's tale and then
He spake with gentle word
Amongst those armèd men :
" I ne'er will pay my wealth,
My people all are free,
We drink King Belé's health,
His subjects ne'er could be.

" His sons I know not then,
But wish they for my gold,
Let them come here like men
And claim it as of old ;
We'll meet them on the strand—
Yet was thy father dear—"
Then beckoned with his hand
His daughter, who sat near.

Then rose the maid in haste
From off her golden chair,
So slender was her waist,
Her bosom was so fair,
The dimples on her cheeks
Young Astrild⁴ oft disclose,
Like a butterfly who takes
His refuge in a rose.

Off to her bower she flees
And brings a purse well spun,
Whereon, 'neath mighty trees,
The beasts of forest run,
And shines the moon's soft light
On sea with ships untold,
Its clasps of rubies bright
With tufts of glittering gold.

She handed it to him,
Her father kind and bold,
Who filled it to the brim,
With foreign coins of gold :
" Take this a gift from me,
Do with it what you will ;
But Frithiof now must stay
Here for the winter chill.

" Courage may oft prevail
Against the winter storms,
But Ham and Hejd ne'er fail
Again to raise their forms.
Ellida may not shoot
Through the dark sea so true,
And many monsters float
The wave, though one ye slew."—

They drank with laughter light
Till upward morn did press,
The golden goblets bright
Brought gladness not excess.
A brimming bumper then
They to Angantyr bare,
And Frithiof with his men
Stayed all the winter there.

XII

FRITHIOF'S RETURN.

AGAIN the sky is bright and blue,
Again the earth is clothed anew.
Frithiof now thanks his host and hastes
Again to plough the watery wastes.
And gladly cuts his swan so black
Through the bright sea her silvery track;
The western wind with spring's soft tongue
Like nightingale above them sung,
And Ægir's daughters in garments blue,
Around the rudder danced and flew.
How sweet it is to turn the bark
From foreign shores, and gladly mark
The smoke curl upward from the spot
Where passed our happy childhood's lot;
The fresh spring yet yon rock doth lave,
But ah! thy father's in the grave,
The faithful maid that pines for thee

Gazes forlorn upon the sea.

Seven days he sailed and not before,

A dark blue streak afar he saw,

On the horizon growing fast,

Till rocks and isles appeared at last.

'Tis his fatherland which now he sees,

Its forests shiver in the breeze,

He hears the rushing waterfall

Dash on the rocks with eddying brawl.

He hails the cape and hails the sound,

And sails beneath the temple round,

Where the last summer many a night,

He'd watched his Ingborg's glimmering light :

" Why comes she not ?   Doth not her soul

Tell her that on the deep I roll?

But perhaps she left her old resort,

And sits forlorn within the court,

And strikes the harp, or weaves the woof."

Now sudden from the temple's roof

His hawk shot up, then downward bore,

To Frithiof's shoulder, as of yore.

And there he flaps his snowy wing,

And none can lure the faithful thing,

With talons scratches without cease,

He gives no rest, he gives no peace,

And bends his beak to Frithiof's ear,

As if he tidings had to bear,
Perchance from Ingeborg renowned,
But none can seize the broken sound.

Ellida now the headland rounds,
Like fawn on grass she blithely bounds,
For well known breakers beat her sides,
Whilst Frithiof glad the bowsprit rides.
He rubs his eyes and lays his hand
Above his brow to see the land;
But though he rubs and views the shore,
He'll find his Framnäs there no more.
The blackened ruins rise in gloom,
Like bones of warriors from a tomb;
Where stood the hall, a desert now,
And ashes whirling round do blow.
Wrathfully Frithiof leapt ashore,
And scanned the desolation o'er,
His father's home a blackened waste.
Now shaggy Bran runs up in haste,
His dog who oft, as brave as good,
Had fought the bear amid the wood;
In many a circle round he sweeps,
And high upon his master leaps.
The milk-white steed with golden mane,
With legs like stag and neck like swan,

On whom so oft had Frithiof sped,
Swept from the vale with springy tread;
Gladly he neighs, his neck he bends,
And waits for bread from Frithiof's hands;
Poor Frithiof, now more poor than they,
Hath nothing more to give away.

Houseless and sad—on his own land,
Gazing around did Frithiof stand,
When aged Hilding met him there,
His foster father with silver hair.
" At what I see, I scarce have wondered,
The eagle flown, his nest is plundered.
A valorous, kingly deed, in troth!
And well King Helgé keeps his oath,
Pursuing men with vengeance gory,
Whilst fire and murder are his glory;
It causes me more wrath than care,
But tell me, where is Ingborg fair?"
" The news I bring," the old man said,
"I fear thou'lt find but little glad.
E'en as you sailed King Ring advanced,
Five shields to one against us glanced,
In Disardal the battle lay,
And blood-red ran the brook that day.
King Halfdan laughed with many a joke,

Yet many a foeman's helmet broke;
I held my shield above the boy,
His courage filled my heart with joy.
Not long the unequal strife we bore,
King Helgé fled, then all was o'er.
The Asar's friend, in wild career,
Kindled thy house whilst passing near.
Then to the kings a summons sped,
To yield at once the lovely maid,
She only could Ring's wrath appease,
If not, both land and crown he'd seize.
On peace at length the kings decide,
And Ring hath ta'en away his bride."

"O woman, woman," Frithiof said,
"The first dark thought that Loké² had,
It was a lie and he sent it then,
In woman's shape to trouble men.
A blue-eyed lie, that with false tears
Always deceives and yet endears;
High bosomed lie so lily fair,
With faith like ice in spring, or air;
Deceit and guile dwell in thy heart,
And quick each tie is torn apart!
Alas, how dear she was to me,
How dear she is, and aye will be!

From childhood's dawn and early day,
She was my mate at sport and play,
No exploit swam before my eyes
But she shone forth the hope and prize.
As trees whose growth has been the same,
And Thor strikes one with lightning flame,
The other withers; blossoms one,
Its mate displays its leaves anon;
Thus were our joys and sorrows past,
'Tis hard to be alone at last.
I am alone.   O mighty Var[3] !
Who round the earth dost travel far,
Of broken vows account to make,
From thy vain labours respite take.
With lies thy tablets soon will fill,
And soon destroyed thy faithful quill ;
Of Balder's Nanna I've heard a tale,
But love in woman's breast is frail,
Faith rests not now on human choice,
Since guile is in my Ingborg's voice—
That voice like Zephyr's waving wings,
Or harp sounds soft from Bragé's strings.
I'll not the sound of harp abide,
I will not think on my faithless bride !
Where the storm roars, there will I be,
Blood shall thou drink, O boundless sea !

Where the sword sows the tomb's fell seed,
There will I glide among the dead,
Meeting perchance a king with his crown,
I'll laugh with joy as I hew him down,
In combat, perhaps, among the rest,
Some stripling with enamoured breast,
A fool, who trusts in love and truth,
For pity's sake I'll fell the youth,
Spare him that one day he may die,
Insulted, scorned, betrayed as I."

" How youth's wild humour onward speeds,"
Said aged Hilding, "how it needs
To be cooled down by age's snow ;
You wrong the noble maiden so.
Complain not of my fosterchild,
But blame the Norna's anger wild,
Unmoved by mortals, but which rains,
Thundering upon us from heaven's plains.
None heard the maiden's wailing song,
Like silent Vidar [4] she bore her wrong ;
Silent she wept, as in laurel grove
Bemoans her mate the turtle dove.
To me she gave her heart relief,
Within it dwells unceasing grief.
As the waterfowl with wounded breast,

Dives in the eddying pool, and lest
The day should on her torture glare,
Lies at the bottom and dies there.
So her crushing woe in darkness slept,
I only know how the brave girl wept.
' I am a sacrifice,' she said,
' For Belé's kingdom, on my head
The snowdrops bloom with evergreens,
But endless woe for me begins.
I might expire, but 'twere in vain,
I should not shun eternal pain;
A lingering death few long endure,
Whose hearts beat high and blood runs pure.
But to no man my grief relate,
I want not pity for my fate,
King Belé's daughter pity spurns,
But Frithiof greet when he returns.'
The bridal morn arrived (whose sun
Its fatal course was doomed to run),
Up to the temple mounted then
Troops of young girls and armèd men.
The singers chanted there indeed,
But pale the bride on her coal black steed,
Pale as a spirit in snow-white shroud
Seated upon a thunder cloud;
From the saddle I lifted my lily tall,

I

And led her up to the temple hall,
The altar round, where she softly said
To Lofn [5] her vows with bended head.
And much to the snow-white one she prayed,
Whilst all did weep, except the maid.
Helgé espied the ring she wore,
Thy ring, which from her arm he tore:
'Tis now hung up in Balder's fane;
No more could I my wrath restrain;
From its sheath I tore my good sword forth,
Not much was then King Helgé worth.
But Ingborg whispered soft, 'Forbear,
A brother might this insult spare,
Let me endure till life be past,
Allfather judge us at the last.' "

"Allfather, judge us," said Frithiof stern,
"But to judge a little myself I yearn.
Is it not Balder's midsummer feast?
In the temple is now the crownèd priest,
The murderous king, who sold my bride,
I also to judge a little decide."

XIII.

BALDER'S FIRE.

THE midnight sun [1] on the mountain lay,
And blood-red was its glare,
It was not night and it was not day,
And dim the murky air.

The fire, fair image of the sun,
Burnt on the holy hearth,
Soon will its flickering flames be done,
And Höder [2] rule the earth.

The priests around the temple stood,
Aged and pale were they,
They stirred and fed the up-piled wood,
Streaming their tresses grey.

The crownèd king in all his power
Near the altar round doth move,
Hark! in the deadly midnight hour,
Clash weapons in the grove.

" Björn, in thy grasp hold fast the door,
Taken is every man,
Hew down upon the marble floor
Each fugitive you scan."

The king became all pale, he knew
The accents bold too well;
Wrathfully Frithiof onward flew,
His voice like storm did swell.

" Here is the red gold which my skiff
Bore from the western isle;
Take it!   Now fight we here for life
Or death by Balder's pile.

" Shield upon back and bare the breast,
We will the combat join;
The first good blow as king thou hast,
But mind, the next is mine.

" Gaze not so eager at the door,
The fox is ta'en in his lair,
Think upon Framnäs' ruin sore,
And sister with yellow hair."

So spake the hero in his wrath,
From his belt the purse did bring,
And little careful he slung it forth,
And struck on the brow the king.

Blood came gushing from the wound,
Darkness before his eye;
Fainting beside the altar round
The Asa friend did lie.

"Countest thou not thy golden gain,
Coward, thy wealth to see?
Angurvadel will never deign,
To slay the like of thee.

" Be still, ye priests with gory knives,
Pale princes of the moon;
Or it may cost your wretched lives,
My blade will thirst full soon.

" Shining Balder, thy wrath disarm,
Nor look so dark on me,
The ring thou bearest on thine arm,
By theft was given to thee.

" For well I ween 'twas not for thee
Forgèd by Vaulund's skill;
Subdued a weeping maid may be,
But away with their cowardly guile ! "

Bravely he tugged, but both arm and ring
Had grown together quite;
When it loosened became, the god did spring
Into the flames from spite.

Hear !   How it crackles, the flames assail
The golden roof and beams,
Björn by the door stands deadly pale,
Even Frithiof to tremble seems.

" Let the people out; ope wide the door;
A guard no more I need.
The temple burns, pour water, pour
The whole sea over with speed ! "

Now from the temple down to the strand,
Are knitted of warriors chains,
The billow passes from hand to hand,
Hisses 'gainst charred remains.

Frithiof stood, like the god of rain,
High on the roof and shot
Water on all around amain,
Calm 'mid the ruins hot.

In vain! Fire gets the upper hand,
The smoke rolls overhead,
The gold drops on the burning sand,
The silver plates burn red.

And all is lost! From the half burnt house,
A fiery cock [3] now springs,
Sits on the temple's roof and crows,
And wildly flaps his wings.

The morning wind now blowing high,
Up 'gainst the sky it blazes,
And Balder's grove is summer dry,
The hungry flame it seizes.

Springing from branch to branch it came
Onward with speed amazing,
Hurrah! What wild, what fearful flame!
How Balder's pile is blazing!

Listen, how crackle the riven roots,
See how the summits flare.
With Muspel's [4] blood-red sons what boots
The power of men compare?

A sea of fire is Balder's ground,
Strandless its waves do swell,
The sun goes up, but fjord and sound
Reflect the flames of hell.

The temple soon in ashes lay,
Ashes the temple's bower;
Wofully Frithiof goes his way,
Weeps in the morning hour.

XIV.

FRITHIOF GOES INTO EXILE.

In galley light,
On summer night,
Sat hero sad.
Like breakers mad
Now care, now wrath
In him burst forth,
Whilst blazing fane
Smoked on amain.

" Dark rolling smoke,
From temple rock,
Valhalla seek,
Let vengeance wreak
The White One's wrath
'Gainst me called forth.
Fly high and shriek,

That heaven may quake,
Of temple round,
Burnt to the ground;
Of image fair
Prostrated there,
Consumed by flame
When down it came.
The forests then,
Secure since men
Bound sword on thigh,
Now burnt do lie,
Accustomed they
To rot away!
This haste to bear
To Balder's ear,
Thou smoky shroud,
To god of cloud!

" Right well they'll sing
The righteous king,
Who banished me,
By his decree,
From out his land.
But on!   We stand
On kingdom blue
Where billows flow.

Thou must not rest,
But thou must haste,
Ellida, fly
Through breakers high;
For thou must roam
On salt sea foam,
My galley good:
A drop of blood
Will often flow
Where'er we go.
'Mid storm and foam
Thou art my home:
Helgé accurst
Hath burnt the first.
Thou art my north,
My foster earth,
Whilst from mine own
Away I've flown:
My bride, all hail,
In pitch black veil;
The one in white
Kept not her plight.

" Thou rolling sea,
Unbounded, free,
No kings oppress

Thy happiness:
Thy king is he
Among the free,
Who never quakes,
Though stormy breaks
The sparkling crest
On foaming breast.
The clear blue wave
Delights the brave;
His vessels plough
Thy fields enow,
And blood-rain showers
'Neath oaken towers,
Steel bright and bare
The seedcorn there.
Thy fields all gory
Bear fruit of glory,
Harvest of gold;
Thou billow old,
Be true to me,
I'll follow thee.
My father's tomb
Lies still in gloom,
With ocean's din
Around its green.
Mine blue shall be,

The foaming sea,
Shall swim for aye
In storm and spray,
And gently flow
In depths below.
To me by heaven
As home thou'rt given;
Thou rolling wave,
Shalt be my grave."

So sang he wild
Whilst, like a child,
He wept to roam
Away from home.
He gently sails
Through rocks and isles,
Which yet do guard
The shallow fjord.
But vengeance wakes;
King Helgé takes
Ten ships of war,
Sails from the shore.
Then shouted all:
"Now king must fall.
A fight he gives;
Now no more thrives

Valhalla's son
Beneath the moon;
Despite his name,
Wherefrom he came,
The king must roam
To Odin home."

Scarce on their course,
An unseen force,
The sharp keel nips
Of Helgé's ships;
And more and more
They downward bore,
To Rana's death,
When out of breath,
King Helgé swam
From sinking stem.

But Björn, the glad,
Laughed loud and said :
" Thou Asa blood,
The trick was good.
Without a word
The ships I bored,
A night ago,
A lawful blow.

Rana, the queen,
As aye hath been,
Kept all that came,
But 'twas a shame,
She did not sink
The king, I think."

In angry mood
King Helgé stood,
His bow he bent,
With fell intent,
Steel forged and round,
'Gainst rocky ground.
He scarcely knew
How hard he drew,
Till with a twang
The arrow sprang.

Lance waving high,
Did Frithiof cry:
" Death eagle bear
I fettered here ;
Did it but fly
Then would the high
King-coward fall
For once and all.

But do not think
My lance would drink
A coward's blood!
'Tis for the good
And for the brave.
On runic grave
It may be seen,
But not, I ween,
On niding stocks,[2]
Where thy name rocks.
These ships of thine
Are 'neath the brine,
Nor is thy hand
Worth more on land.
Rust breaketh steel,
Not thou; I deal
My vengeance stern
When I return.
Beware! lest dread
It strike thy head."

He seized a fir,
Fashioned as oar,
A mast-fir grown
In valley lone.
He seized its mate

And rowing sate.
He rows with speed;
Like bending reed,
The oars do dash
With feathery splash.

The sun goes up
From mountain top,
The whispering wind
Doth soft remind
The wave to dance
In morning glance.
On billow tops
Ellida hops
With joy along,
But Frithiof sung :

" World-circle's brow,
Thou mighty North !
I may not go
Upon thine earth;
But in no other
I love to dwell,
Now, hero-mother,
Farewell, farewell !

" Farewell, thou high
And heavenly one,
Night's sleeping eye,
Midsummer sun.
Thou clear blue sky,
Like hero's soul,
Ye stars on high,
Farewell, farewell.

" Farewell, ye mounts,
Where Honour thrives,
And Thor recounts
Good warriors' lives.
Ye azure lakes,
I know so well,
Ye woods and brakes,
Farewell, farewell !

" Farewell, ye tombs,
By billow blue,
The lime tree blooms
Its snow on you.
The Saga[3] sets
In judgment well
What earth forgets ;
Farewell, farewell.

" Farewell the heath,
The forest hoar,
I played beneath,
By streamlet's roar.
To childhood's friends,
Who loved me well,
Remembrance sends
A fond farewell!

" My love is foiled,
My rooftree rent,
Mine honour soiled,
In exile sent!   ·
We turn from earth,
On ocean dwell,
But, joy and mirth,
Farewell, farewell! "

XV

THE VIKING'S CODE.

Now he wandered about on the salt desert waste, like
    prey-seeking falcon he flew ;
But for warriors on board he wrote maxims and rules.
    Wilt list to the laws of his crew?

"Not a tent upon deck, and no sleeping ashore, within
    houses but enemies go;
Vikings sleep on their shields with their swords in their
    hands, and for tent have they heaven the blue.

" Short the hammer's strong haft of victorious Thor, but
    an ell long Frey's falchion is made,
'Tis enough, hast thou heart, grip thine enemy close, and
    then long enough is the blade.

" When wild hurricanes rage, hoist the sail high above, it
        is blithe on the rough rolling deep ;
Let her drive, let her drive, he who strikes is afraid, and
        I'd rather beneath the sea sleep.

" Maids are safe upon land, and they come not on board;
        were she Freya she would thee ensnare :
On her cheek the fair dimples are traps for the brave
        and a net is her long flowing hair.

" Wine is Valfather's drink, and a bout is allowed, pro-
        vided with judgment you drink.
He who reels upon land can arise, but to Ran to the
        sleep-giver here would you sink.

" When the merchant ye meet, ye may spare his good
        ship, but the weaker his wealth must unfold.
Thou art king on thy wave, he is slave of his gain, and
        thy steel is as good as his gold.

" For the booty on deck with lots may ye cast, how they
        fall out ye may not complain ;
But the sea-king himself will ne'er cast a lot, but only
        the honour retain.

" When the enemy comes and there's conflict and strife,
    and hot fall the blows on the shields ;
If thou waver'st a step, from among us depart; 'tis our
    law for the niding who yields.

" When victorious, be mild; he who begs for his life, bears
    no sword, cannot be thy foe.
Prayer is Valhalla's child, hear the pale one's voice ; he
    is niding who says to him no.

" Vikings' glory, a wound, adorning its man when on
    bosom or forehead its lies.
Let it bleed, bind it not before twenty four hours, and
    maybe 'fore spring you will rise."

So these laws he gave forth, and his name with each day
    waxed famous on foreign domain,
He found not his equal on dark rolling sea, and his men
    fought with might and main.

By the rudder he sat, and dark did he look as he gazed
    at the bottomless sea :
" Thou art deep ; in thy depths perhaps some peace may
    be found, but above them it never can be.

"Is the White One enraged? let him take his bright
      sword, I will perish if so he resolve;
But he sits in the clouds, and reflections sends down
      which in darkness my spirit involve."

Yet when combat was near, then his dark mood took
      flight and bold as an eagle he rose,
And his forehead is bright and clear is his voice, like the
      Thunderer he stands up 'gainst foes.

So from conquest to conquest still onward he swept, he
      was safe on the wide foaming grave ;
And he saw in the South both the isles and the rocks,
      sailing by on the Grecian wave.

When he saw the dark laurels arise from the deep with
      the tottering temple above,
What he thought Freya knows, and the Skalds know it
      too, and ye know it, ye beings who love.

"Here we should have abode, here the isle, here the grove,
      and the temple my sire shadowed forth.
It was here, it was here, I implored her to come, but the
      cruel one stayed in the North!

"Dwells not peace in those far distant valleys above,
    dwells not mem'ry those columns among?
And like lovers' soft whispers the murmuring brook, and
    like love-chant the nightingale's song?

"Where is Ingeborg now? For the gray-haired old
    king have all kind remembrances flown?
Ah! I cannot forget, and I'd give up my life to see her,
    to see her alone!

"And three years have passed by since I saw my dear
    land, the home of the Sagas so deep.
Strike the glorious mountains the heavens still? Is it
    green where my forefathers sleep?

"On the tomb where my father is laid have I planted
    a lime-tree; ah! doth she live now?
Who watches the sapling? O earth, give thy sap, and thy
    dew, O high heaven, give thou!

"Yet why wander I thus far away from my home, take
    booty, and slay warriors bold?
I have glory enough, and my spirit abhors the paltry and
    glittering gold.

" See the flag on the mast, how it points to the North, to
    the North my fatherland dear,
I will follow the path of the heavenly wind and straight
    for the North will I steer ! "

XVI

FRITHIOF AND BJÖRN.

—◆—

FRITHIOF.

Björn, I am wearied of ocean's wrath,
On the tossing billow no rest is found,
I long to return and to gaze around
On the mighty fells of belovéd North.
O happy he who ne'er left his home,
Ne'er has been chased from his forefathers' graves ;
Already too long, too long do I roam
Restless around on the salt sea waves.

BJÖRN.

Blame not the sea, for true is its breast,
Freedom and happiness dwell on the seas,
Nothing they know of luxurious ease,
But love on the ocean for ever to rest.

When I am old, on the fresh verdant earth
Will I also grow on as firm as a tree,
Now will I battle and revel in mirth,
Now shall my life be both careless and free.

FRITHIOF.

Hunted by ice are we now to ground,
Lifeless the waves round our good keel blend,
Winter the tedious I care not to spend
Here among rocks to this desert bound.
Yuletide once more in the North will I dare,
Visit King Ring and my childhood's choice,
Yet again gaze on her yellow hair,
Once more will hear her melodious voice.

BJÖRN.

Good ; I am with thee ; and King Ring shall learn
Ruthless the vengeful viking's power,
Singe the old king at the midnight hour,
Sweep off the fair one, the castle burn ;
Or it may be that in vikings' wise
Singly to combat the king you will call,
Or summon his forces to fight on the ice ;
Say what you will; I am ready for all.

FRITHIOF.

Name not destruction nor think upon strife,
Peacefully thither my course do I steer ;
Ring hath not sinned nor his queen without peer,
Vengeance divine hath blasted my life ;
Nothing remains on the earth but gloom,
Farewell will I say to her I hold dear,
Farewell for ever !   When forests do bloom,
Perchance before that I again shall be here.

BJÖRN.

Frithiof, thy folly I ne'er will permit,
Sighing and grief for the sake of a maiden,
Earth, save the mark, is with women o'erladen,
Thousands you'll find should you one chance to quit.
Speak, and I'll fetch you a cargo for gold,
Fresh from the South, of young maidens fair,
Gentle and tender as lambs in the fold—
For these we'll draw lots or as brothers share.

FRITHIOF.

Björn, you are open and gladsome as Frey,
Bold in the battle and prudent in troth,
Odin and Thor, you may know them both ;
Freya the heavenly, you know not her way.

Judge not the gods nor their influence dire ;
Recklessly waken not fair Freya's rage ;
Sooner or later her slumbering fire
Burns with a fury that nought can assuage.

BJÖRN.

Go not alone then, beware of the king.

FRITHIOF.

Friendless I go not, my sword is with me.

BJÖRN.

Mind'st thou how Hagbart was hanged on a tree ?

FRITHIOF.

He who is taken deserves to swing.

BJÖRN.

Fall'st thou, strife-brother, like death-eagle fell,
Vengeance I'll take for Frithiof's stock !

FRITHIOF.

'Tis useless, Björn ; for the crowing cock
Hears he no longer than I ; farewell.

XVII

FRITHIOF VISITS KING RING.

———•———

KING RING he sat at his yuletide feast, and quaffed his
    mead and ale ;
And by him sat his youthful queen, like lily fair and
    pale.
If spring and autumn thus conjoined and hand in hand
    might be,
She were the fresh and gladsome spring, the chilly
    autumn he.

But lo ! within the lofty hall a strange old man strode in;
From head to foot his stalwart form was clothed in
    swarthy skin.
He bore a staff within his hand, his shape was slightly
    bent,
Yet taller far than those around that ancient stranger
    went.

He sat himself upon the bench hard by the great hall
    door—
Here are the places for the poor, as they have been before;
The courtiers laughed contemptuously, and whispered
    man to man,
And pointed with the finger at the bowed-down bear-
    skin man.

Like lightning flashed the stranger's eyes, like lightning
    bright and clear,
With one strong hand he seized a youth who thus stood
    smiling near ;
With ease he took the courtier up and on the ground
    he threw ;
The others then were silent—we should have been so too.

" What ho ! who makes this uproar?   Who thus our
    peace doth break ?
Come up to me, thou old man, and let us with thee speak.
What is thy name ?   What wilt thou ?   Thy country let
    us know."
Thus spake the king in anger to the old man down
    below.

" Thou wishest much to know, O king; but I will answer
    thee ;

My name alone I shall withhold—'t belongs alone to me.
At Aanger was I nurtured, but Brist men call my home ;
I dwelt some time with Ulven—from him I now am
    come.

" Of yore I rode so glad and safe upon a dragon strong ;
Like rushing wind from mountain side he boldly swept
    along ;
He now lies lame and frozen in a far distant land ;
Myself, old, helpless, ailing, burn salt upon the strand.

" I came to see thy wisdom, so far and wide displayed ;
They met me here with laughter—for that I am not
    made.
I seized a fool and shook him, and away from me did
    fling ;
Quite safe and sound he rose again ; forgive me this,
    King Ring."

" In sooth," replied the monarch, " I find thy words are
    just,
For men should honour silver locks. Come, sit by me
    thou must.
Let fall thy cumbrous bearskin and let me scan thy face.
Disguise suits ill with gladness but joy my board shall
    grace.

Now from the old man's stooping head is loosed the
    sable hood,
When lo ! a young man smiling stands, where erst the
    old one stood.
See ! From his lofty forehead, round shoulders broad
    and strong,
The golden locks flow glistening, like sunlight waves
    along.

He stood before them glorious in velvet mantle blue,
His baldrics broad, with silver worked, the artist's skill
    did shew ;
For round about the hero's breast and round about his
    waist,
The beasts and birds of forest wild embossed each other
    chased.

The armlet's yellow lustre shone rich upon his arm ;
His war-sword by his side—in strife a thunderbolt alarm.
Serene the hero cast his glance around the men of war ;
Bright stood he there as Balder, as tall as Asa Thor.

As when the Northern Lights appear and gild the snowy
    peak,
So glowed the changeful colour on the startled lady's
    cheek ;

As when twin water-lilies, contesting 'gainst the storm,
Bend, heaving with each wavelet, so heaved her bosom
    warm.

The trumpet's blast resounded; deep silence greets its
    sound,
Now is the hour of promise come ; Frey's boar is borne
    around,
With chaplets round his shoulders, an apple 'twixt his
    teeth,
And four stout knees he bended upon the dish beneath.

King Ring he started from his seat, and streamed his
    tresses gray,
He touched the wild boar's forehead, and thus with oath
    did say :
" I swear to capture Frithiof, though proved in many a
    war,
So help me Frey and Odin, also the mighty Thor."

With scornful laughter rose again the stranger guest so
    tall—
Heroic wrath flashed o'er his face ; he eyed them one and
    all,
With sword-hilt smote the table—the hall resounding
    rang ;

Up from his oak bench instantly each gallant warrior
    sprang.

" And listen now," quoth he, " sir king, whilst I my vow
    do tell,
Young Frithiof is my firmest friend—certes, I know him
    well ;
I swear to fight for Frithiof, for him and for his weal;
So help me thou, my Norna, also my faithful steel."

The king replied with laughter loud: " Though bold
    thy speech may be,
Within a Northern court 'tis known that words go ever
    free.
Fill him the flowing horn, my queen, with wine of all
    the best,
This winter, may I hope, the knight will tarry here our
    guest."

The queen she took the goblet up, and forward gently
    came ;
(The cup was made of wild bull's skull, adorned with
    many a gem ;
It stood on silver pedestal, with golden circlets bound,
Carved o'er with ancient figures, and runic letters
    round).

With downcast eye she took the cup and proffered it
     alone,
But, lo! the hand is trembling, and wine is spilt
     thereon.
As purple sunset reddens deep the sky, the sea, the
     land,
So burnt the dark drops crimson upon her snow-white
     hand.

Now gladly took the guest the horn up from the noble
     dame,·
Not two of us could drain it; men are not now the
     same;
But quick, and without winking, to please the lovely
     queen,
The mighty hero drained it without a breath between.

Then touched the skald his harpstrings, close by the
     monarch's side,
And sang of love which true and fast doth in the North
     abide,
Of Hagbart and sweet Signé, till his deep measured
     tone
Through adamantine corslets softened those hearts of
     stone.

He sang the halls of Valhalla and the Einheris'[1] gain,
Of glorious fathers' deeds of might on field and foaming
   main;
Then seized each hand the falchion, and flamed each
   rolling eye,
And quickly filled and emptied ranged the goblet
   passing by.

Now all had drunk their fill and more within the royal
   house,
Each warrior that Yuletide night did royally carouse.
Then went he on his way to rest with neither wrath
   nor care,
But old King Ring slept peacefully beside his partner
   fair.

XVIII.

THE JOURNEY ON THE ICE.

ON a visit King Ring with his queen will pass
O'er the ice-covered sea, like polished glass.

"Go not on the ice," the stranger saith;
"It will break, and deep is the chilly bath."

"Kings drown not so easily," Ring did say,
"But he who's afraid may go round the bay."

The stranger he looked so dark at the joke,
And quick on his feet the skates did yoke.

The sledge-horse sweeps with might away,
His breath is in flame, he is so gay.

"Stretch out," cried the king, "my courser good,
Show whether thou art of Sleipnir's [1] blood."

They sweep like a storm-cloud thro' the air,
The old man regards not his partner's prayer.

But the steel-shod warrior, he stands not still,
But passes them by whenever he will.

Full many a rune on the ice he cut,
Fair Ingeborg over her name doth shoot.

So haste they away o'er the slippery path,
But underneath lurks false Ran in wrath.

A hole in her silver roof she clove,
And quickly the sledgers into it drove.

Fair Ingeborg's cheeks became all pale,
But the guest he came like a whirling gale.

Deep in the ice his skates he placed,
And seized the courser's mane in haste.

Then up on the ice one single haul
Soon landed both sledge, and horse, and all.

"The feat must I praise," did the king exclaim,
"Only Frithiof the strong could have done the same."

Then back to the castle they took their ways;
And the stranger remained till Spring's fair days.

XIX

FRITHIOF'S TEMPTATION.

———♦———

Spring now comes with chirping birds, and budding
  leaves and laughing sun,
And the streams, released from Winter, surging down to
  Occan run.
Blushing bright as beauteous Freya, peeps from out its
  bud the rose,
And in human hearts and bosoms love of life and courage
  glows.

Now the aged king will hunt, the queen will with him in
  the chace,
And the Court in motley splendour over hill and valley
  race ;
Bows are jingling, quivers rattle, chargers paw the
  ground away,
And with hood upon his forehead shrieks the falcon for
  his prey.

Soo! the queen approaches lightly (wretched Frithiof,
    look not there !)
Like the morning star in spring time glitt'ring in the
    misty air.
Half like Freya, half like Rota, fairer far than both the
    two,
From the graceful purple bonnet lightly float the feathers
    blue.

Look not on her eye's blue heaven, look not on her
    yellow hair,
Caution, for her waist is slender ; caution, for her breast
    is fair !
Gaze not on the rose and lily changeful blooming on her
    face,
Hear not those beloved accents, whispering like the
    evening breeze !

Now the hunting troop is ready ! Hurrah, over hill
    and dale !
Trumpets echo, falcon soaring straight 'gainst Odin's
    home doth sail,
Beasts of forest fly in terror, seek in haste their secret
    home,
After them, with spear-head levelled, the Valkyria doth
    come.

Aged king can hardly follow cavalcade in headlong
    chace,

Lonely by his side rides Frithiof, silent he with serious
    face.

Dark and painful thoughts are surging in his bosom
    bold and strong,

And where'er reflection wanders, hears he still their
    wailing song :

"Mighty Ocean wherefore left I, for my danger madly
    blind ?

Billows drive away reflection, blown away by heaven's
    wind.

Broods the viking, cometh danger, bids him to the
    dangerous dance,

And the racking tortures vanish, charmed away by
    weapon's glance.

"Different here I find my temper, boundless passion
    tears my soul,

Strikes her wings upon my forehead, in a dream I
    onward roll ;

Can I banish from my mem'ry midnight vows, affiance
    sworn ?

Vanished treasures—she ne'er broke them—vengeful
    gods my soul have torn.

" Oh they hate humanity, and scatter grief on joy with
    zest,
Stole away my youthful rosebud, placed it in cold
    Winter's breast ;
What doth Winter chill with rosebuds ?   Can he under-
    stand their price ?
No ! his cold unthankful spirit clothes both bud and
    stalk in ice."

Thus he sang with plaintive voice. They soon approached
    a lonely dell,
Dark, enclosed by lofty mountains, shaded o'er by birches
    well.
Then the king in haste dismounted, said : " How fair,
    how cool the bower,
I am tired, my soul is weary, I will slumber here an
    hour."

" Sleep not, king, for cold the ground, and hard to lay
    the weary brow,
Heavy sleep will little help thee.   Up ! and to the castle
    go."—
" Sleep, like other god-like beings, comes upon us un-
    awares,
Let the old man for a moment here repose his silver
    hairs."

Frithiof then took off his mantle, on the mossy turf he
   spread,
On his knee the aged monarch gently laid his weary
   head ;
Gently slept he as the warrior after battle's stern
   alarms
On his shield ; as sleeps the infant quiet in its mother's
   arms.

As he slumbers, list ! a raven croaks from out the neighbouring brake :
" Haste thee, Frithiof, kill the old man, for thy suff'ring
   vengeance take.
Take his queen, for she is thine—to thee the bridal kiss
   she gave,
Not a mortal eye beholds thee, silent is the darksome
   grave."

Frithiof listens, hear ! there warbles snow-white dove
   from out the brake :
" Though no mortal eye behold thee, Odin's eye doth
   record make.
Niding, wilt thou kill the sleeper ? the defenceless old
   man slay ?
Great your gain, but hero's scutcheon never more on
   earth display ! "

Thus in varied strain they sang. But Frithiof seized
    his war-sword good,
Flung it forth with horror from him, deep into the
    darksome wood.
Coal-black raven flies to Nastrand[1], but on pinion light
    and soft,
Flies the other up to heaven, warbling music sweet
    aloft.

Now the aged king arises : "Much I thank thee for the
    rest,
Sweet is sleep in forest glade, protected by the hero's
    breast.
But where is thy falchion, stranger ? Lightning's
    brother, where is he ?
Who hath parted those who never more in life should
    parted be ? "

Frithiof said : " Full many a blade of equal worth all
    idle lies.
King, the falchion's tongue is pointed, speaketh not in
    peaceful guise. .
Evil spirits dwell in iron, spirits flown from Niffel-
    hem,
Slumber is not sacred for them, silver tresses anger
    them."

" Frithiof, sleep I feigned to prove thee, try thy inmost
 soul alone,
Man and steel, untried in battle, rest the prudent not
 upon.
Thou art Frithiof, I have known thee quickly through
 thy rough disguise,
Old King Ring hath long discovered what his prudent
 guest denies.

" Wherefore crept you to my dwelling, deep disguised,
 with covered face ?
Wherefore but to steal the maiden from the aged king's
 embrace ?
Honour, Frithiof, comes not darkly within hospitable
 law,
As the sun her shield is spotless, and her scutcheon
 without flaw.

" Rumour mentioned of a Frithiof, bane of men and
 heaven's dread,
Shields he clove and temple burnt, as brave as desperate,
 overhead.
Soon he comes, so thought I then, to devastate and spoil
 my land,
And he came, but wrapt in tatters, with a beggar's staff
 in hand.

" Wherefore downcast is thy visage ? I had youth and
    strength before,
Life is but a tedious battle, youth is e'er its Berserk
    hour.
Youth must press 'mid clashing shields, the while its
    boiling rage is hot,
I have suffered and forgiven, dearly loved and then
    forgot.

" See you, I am old and ailing, soon will mount into the
    tomb,
Stranger, take my queen and kingdom when the fatal
    hour is come.
Here remain an honoured guest, and 'neath my royal roof
    a son,
Swordless champion shall defend me, and our ancient
    strife be done."

" Never," answered Frithiof, darkly, " came I here a thief
    to thee,
Would I rob thee of thy consort, tell me who should
    hinder me ?
But my bride again I would behold, once more her
    features view,
Oh ! I madden, half-quenched fires light up devouring
    flames anew !

"Some time in thy hall I dwelt, no more stay I there,
    king.
Gods unreconciled upon me angry thunderbolts do
    fling.
Balder with the golden tresses, he who holds each mortal
    dear,
See, his hate is pointed at me, turned away his face
    severe.

"Yes, I set in flames his temple ; Varg i Veum [2] am
    proclaimed,
Gladness flies the festal meeting, children shriek when I
    am named.
Me my foster earth in anger from her bosom forth hath
    cast,
Without peace within my country, restless care devours
    my breast.

" On green earth no more I wander, vainly seek for rest
    and peace ;
Burns the ground beneath my footsteps, shadeless are the
    barren trees ;
Ingeborg is lost for ever, she from me by Ring was
    ta'en ;
Now in life my sun is quenchèd, only darkness doth
    remain.

M

" Therefore, home unto my breakers.   Hurrah ! out my
        galley good !
Bathe again thy pitch-black bosom gaily in the briny
        flood,
Raise thy spreading wings to heaven, through the hissing
        ocean tear,
Fly so long as stars conduct thee, fly so long as billows
        bear !

" Let me hear the storm's deep thunder, let me see the
        lightning dart ;
When it rages round about me, then 'tis peace in
        Frithiof's heart.
Din of shields and showers of arrows !   On the sea the
        battle lies,
And I fall by gods forgiven, gladly to Valhalla rise."

XX

KING RING'S DEATH.

—◆—

YELLOW-MANED teams,
Shining their hair,
Draw from the wave sun more bright than before.
Morning's sweet beams,
Doubly as fair,
Play in the king's hall.—They knock at the door.

Frithiof brave
Enters forlorn,
Pale sat the king ; and fair Ingeborg's breast
Heaves like a wave.
Sorrowful morn !
Trembling with anguish takes leave the guest.

" Dark billows gush
Round wingèd steed,

Sea-horse away from the haven must wend.
Out will I rush,
Now guest must speed
Off from the land and his trusty friend.

" Ingborg, for ever
This ring I bestow,
Holy remembrances in it remain.
From it ne'er sever,
Frithiof must go ;
Never on earth wilt thou see him again.

" Ne'er will my age
Repose in the North ;
There can I dwell not ; there man is a slave ;
Nornas do rage,
I must go forth,
Range o'er the ocean, my home and my grave.

" Approach not the strand,
Ring, with thy queen,
Most when the stars shed their light o'er the bay.
Perhaps on the sand,
Yellow their sheen,
O'er the wrecked corpse of the Viking may play."

Then quoth the king :
" Hard 'tis to hear
Warrior who weeps like a sorrowing maid.
Death-song doth ring
Deep in mine ear,
Man that is born in the tomb must be laid.

" Nornas decide
Whate'er the stake,
Destiny evenly onward doth run.
Take then thy bride,
My kingdom take,
Keep it in charge for my growing son.

" Friendship I sought,
Seated by board ;
Dearly I loved that peace should prevail.
Yet have I fought,
Cloven spear and sword,
Pierced shields at sea, and never waxed pale.

" Now the red vein
Carve I with spear,
Straw-death becomes not a king in the North.
Little the pain

Now doth appear,
Care not for life—'tis of little worth."

Bravely he slashes
Odin's red letters,
Blood-runes of heroes, on arm and on breast.
Brightly the splashes
Of life's flowing fetters
Drip from the silver of hair-covered chest.

" Bring me the horn !
Hail to thy kind,
Hail to thy mem'ry, thou glorious North !
Ripening corn,
Generous mind,
Peaceful exploit, have I loved upon earth.

" Peace among wild,
Blood-seeking kings
Vainly I sought for ; she fled far away.
Now comes the mild
Goddess, and brings
Peace in the tomb after life's dark day.

" Hail to ye, gods !
Valhalla sons !

Vanishes earth; to the Asa's high feast
Piercing horn bids;
Happiness crowns,
Fair, like a helmet of gold, the new guest!"

Gently he pressed
Ingeborg's hand,
Hand upon son and on weeping friend lain.
Softly to rest,
Spirit so grand
Fled with a sigh to Allfather again.

XXI

RING'S DEATH-SONG.

——◆——

IN the tomb sitting
High born old chieftain,
Sword by his side and
Shield upon arm.
Mettlesome charger
Neighing within it,
Scrapeth with pale hoof
Ground-enclosed grave.

Now rideth mighty
Ring over Bifrost,[1]
Shakes from the burden,
Bending the bridge ;
Up spring Valhalla's
Wide vaulted portals,

Hands of the Asas
Hanging in his.

Thor is not heavenwards,
Warfare he wages;
Valfather motions
Forward the cup.
Corn plaiteth Frey round
Crown of the monarch,
Frigg bindeth azure
Blossoms thereon.

Bragé, that ancient,
Strikes now the gold strings,
Sweeter now murmurs
Song than before.
List'ning reposes
Vanadis[2] radiant,
Bosom 'gainst table,
Burns whilst she hears.

" High sing the war-sword
Dreadful on helmets;
Billows of red blood
Constantly shed.

Strength, of the mighty
Gods the fair birthright,
Fierce as a Berserk
Bites the round shield.

" Dear to us therefore
Was the good king, who
Placed his strong shield o'er
Cottager's field ;
Wisdom and force's
Fairest conception
Mounts as an off'ring
Up to the sky.

" Words full of wisdom
Valfather loves when
Seated by Saga,[3]
Söquabäck's maid.
So rang the king's words
Like Mimer's billows,
Clear and resplendent,
Deep too as they.

" Peacefully settles
Forseti [4] quarrels,

Ruler by Urda's
Dark-heaving wave.
So sat at judgment
Idolized monarch,
Fierce hands united,
Blood-vengeance quelled.

" King was no niggard ;
Round him he scattered,
' Daylight of dwarfs,' and
' Fierce dragon's bed.' [5]
Glad went the gift from
Generous spirit,
Quick from the kind lips
Comfort to woe.

" Welcome, then, wise old
Heir to Valhalla !
Long in the bleak North
Praised be thy name.
Bragé now greets thee,
Courteous with wine draught,
Sent by the Nornas
Down from the North."

XXII

THE KING-ELECTION.

To court! To court! The summon's call
Doth echoing ring.
King Ring is dead! Now gather all
To choose a king.

The peasant takes his sword from ledge—
The steel is blue—
With finger proves the eager edge,
It bites full true.

With gladness look the boys upon
The steel-blue sheen.
Two raise the sword which had for one
Too heavy been.

The daughter scours the helmet clean,
Bright shall it shine—
But blushes deep, for she has seen
Her face therein.

And last he takes the buckler round,
A sun of blood.
All hail!   Free man and iron-bound,
Thou peasant good!

Our country's honour grows from out
Thy bosom strong.
In strife thou art our bulwark stout,
In peace our tongue.

So gather they with warlike cry,
And arms of proof,
In open court, and heaven's sky
Their only roof.

But Frithiof stands upon the stone,
And with him there
The royal boy, a little one
With flaxen hair.

A murmur then on high arose :—
" Too young by far ;
The boy can neither fight our foes,
Nor make our law ! "

But Frithiof on his shoulders broad
Lifted the boy :
" Ye Northmen, see your rightful lord,
Your country's joy.

" See here the race of Odin old,
So fair and free ;
On shield he is as light and bold
As fish in sea.

" I will defend him and his right
With sword and spear,
And set the father's circlet bright
Upon his heir.

" Forseti, Balder's mighty son,
Hath heard my vow ;
And if I leave my task undone,
Strike he me low ! "

High on the shield the boy sat there,
Like king on throne,
Or eagle young, who from his lair
Looks at the sun.

At this delay his youthful blood
Appeared to creep ;
So with one bound on earth he stood,
A royal leap !

Then high the peasants round did sing :—
" We warriors steeled
Elect thee ; be thou like King Ring,
Youth borne on shield !

" Let Frithiof manage thine estate,
Till thou art grown.
Earl Frithiof, let it be thy fate
The queen to own."

But Frithiof darkly frowned : " To-day
A king elect ;
No wedding 'tis ; my bride I may
Myself select.

" To Balder's temple must I hie,
And busy be
With vengeful Nornas there, who cry
Out constantly.

" A moment will I lonely see
The maids with shields[1] ;
They build beneath Time's ancient tree[2]
On verdant fields.

" The fair-haired Balder's outraged fane
My breast doth chide ;
He took, and he must give again
My heart's fair bride."

The new-made king he greeted there,
Kissed on the brow,
And slowly o'er the heather fair
Did silent go.

FRITHIOF ON HIS FATHER'S TOMB.

— ◆ —

" How brightly laughs the sun, how gladly hops
The friendly beam away from bough to bough !
Allfather's glance reflected in dew-drops,
As o'er the ocean spreads the ruddy glow !
Now crimson colours he the mountain tops !
O 'tis the blood which doth to Balder flow !
Soon will the earth in darkness buried be,
Soon sinks he, like a golden shield, in sea.

" First let me therefore those dear spots perceive,
My childhood's darling haunts I cherished so.
Ah ! the same flowers yet scent the air at eve,
And the same birds yet in the forest go.
The ocean yet against the rocks doth heave —
O that it never there did moaning flow !
Of fame and glory aye the false one sings,
And far away from home's delights she brings.

"I know thee well, thou flood, who often bore
The hardy swimmer on thy billow clear.
I know thee, valley, where we fondly swore
Eternal faith, which earth doth never bear.
Ye birches, too, whose bark I once did score
With many a letter, still your forms ye rear !
With silver stems and circling crowns arranged,
All as before, and only I am changed !

"All as before ?   But where are Framnäs' halls,
And Balder's temple on the sacred strand ?
Ah ! it was lovely in my childhood's vales,
But since thereover have passed sword and brand ;
Now rage divine with human vengeance calls
To wand'rers from a black and desert land.
'Thou pious pilgrim, hither do not roam,
For beasts of forest dwell in Balder's home.'

" A tempter haunts us through this life's career,
The dreadful Nidhögg from the world of Hel :
He hates the light divine which shineth clear
Upon the hero's brow, or spotless steel.
Each hateful deed the hour of wrath doth bear,
That is his work and bears the demon's seal ;
And when he sees the temple burning stands,
Then claps he joyously his coal black hands.

" Is there no pardon then in Valhall's hall ?
O blue-eyed Balder, are there no amends ?
Amends take men, if haply friends should fall ;
And man to God the sweet peace off'ring sends.
'Tis said thou art the mildest god of all,
Command the off'ring which thy wrath unbends.
Thy shrine's destruction was not Frithiof's aim ;
Remove the blot from off his shield of fame.

" Take off thy burden, which I cannot bear,
Crush in my soul the demon's darksome spell ;
Despise me not, but let my honour fair
Appease thine anger dire, though once I fell ;
I blench not though the Thund'rer's self stood near,
I dare stand face to face with pallid Hel ;
Thou pious god, that like the moonbeam glancest,
Thee only fear I, and the bolts thou launchest.

" Here is my father's tomb.   The hero sleeps !
Ah ! he rode off whence none e'er come away.
How dwells he, say they, where the bright star sweeps,
And quaffs his mead and joins in the affray.
Thou heavenly guest ! look down from heaven's steeps,
Thy son, O Thorsten Vikingsson, doth pray !
I come not here with witchcraft or with charms ;
But teach me to return to Balder's arms.

"Has the tomb then no tongue ?   Angantyr tall
Cried from the grave but lately for a blade.
That sword was good, but Tirsing's price was small
'Gainst what I ask, though sword I never prayed ;
Swords capture I in single fight ; but all
I ask from thee is help and godlike aid.
My hazy eye and groping step guide forth,
A noble temper bears not Balder's wrath.

"What ! silent, father ?   Hear the dashing wave,
Light in its murmur let thine answer fly.
The storm with loosened wings doth onward rave,
Whisp'ring unto me, sweep upon it by.
The sun the clouds with golden light doth lave,
Let one of them to me as herald cry.—
No word, no token for thy son in need
Can'st give, my father ?   O how poor the dead !"

The sun is quenched, the evening zephyr sings
For earth's sad child from heaven its lullaby,
And crimson sunset rises up and brings
Its rosy chariot round the burning sky,
O'er purple vales and purple mountains flings
Her glowing mantle, heavenly canopy,
When sudden o'er the western wave there came
A form which rustled on in gold and flame.

A hägring[1] call we this Valhalla wonder,
(But there indeed its name more sweet had been,)
It floateth gently o'er the forest yonder,
A golden crown upon a bed of green.
Above it glitters and it glitters under,
And shines with splendour weird before not seen.
At length it stopped and earthwards did incline,
And where the temple stood, is now a shrine.

Image of Breidablick[2], the lofty wall
Stood silver-bright upon the rock and shone,
Of deep blue steel designed each pillar tall,
And altar round composed of precious stone ;
As if of spirits borne, each pinnacle
Hung like a wintry sky with pure stars sown,
And high therein in mantles blue were found,
Valhalla's gods with golden circlets crowned.

And lo ! reclining on their runic shields
The mighty Nornas now the portal fill ;
Three rosebuds fair which the same garden yields,
With aspect serious, but charming still.
Whilst Urda points upon the blackened fields,
The fairy temple Skulda doth reveal.
When Frithiof first his dazzled senses cleared,
Rejoiced, admired, the vision disappeared.

"I comprehend, O maids from Mimer bright,
This was thy token, hero-father good !
I will restore the ravished temple's site,
Fair on the precipice where erst it stood.
O 'tis a glorious blessing to requite
With peaceful actions youth's hot haughty mood.
Within this downcast bosom hope now lives,
Since the white god my former sins forgives.

"Welcome, ye stars, that gleaming march on high !
Now gladly gaze I on your silent way.
Welcome, ye northern lights, and blood-red sky !
To me a burning shrine but yesterday.
Grave of my fathers, bloom ! and, ocean, sigh
Out sweetly as before thy mournful lay !
Here will I sleep upon my shield and dream
How pious deeds the sins of youth redeem."

XXIV.

THE RECONCILIATION.

———•———

COMPLETED now was Balder's temple; and around
A wooden barrier stood not now, but palings made
Of hammered iron were raised, with spikes of burnished
     gold,
Round Balder's shrine, as if a steel-clad, armèd host,
With halberts and with golden helm upraised, kept watch,
Standing on silent guard round Balder's new abode.
Of giant stones alone its circle wide was built,
With cunning art united—a stupendous work,
Made to defy decay, like to Upsala's temple,
Where the North sees Valhalla in an earthly shape.
Proud stood it there upon the lofty cliff, and mirrored
Its haughty forehead in the ocean's sunny wave;
But round about, like to a gorgeous bed of flowers,
Stretched Balder's dales, encumbered thick with mur-
     muring groves,

With all their warbling birds—a smiling home of peace.
High were the brazen portals, and disclosed within
Two colonnades, upon whose mighty shoulder-blades
Rested the oval dome; and there it hung so fair
Over the temple, like a shield embossed with gold.
But further stood the altar; it was carvèd from
A single northern marble block; and all around
Snakes twined their knotted forms, engraved with runic
      lore,
Deep-pondered words from Vala and from Havamal.[1]
But in the wall above was seen a spacious niche,
With golden stars upon a dark-blue ground; and there
The silver image of the pious god sat mild
And kind, as sits the moon upon the vault of heaven;
So shone the temple glorious. Two and two stepped in
Twelve sacred maidens, all arrayed in silver gauze,
With roses on their healthful cheeks, and roses in
Their guileless hearts. Before the image of the god
They danced the newly consecrated altar round,
As the spring breezes lightly o'er the rivulet,
As fairies of the woods dance in the waving grass,
When in the morning dew lies glittering thereon.
And 'mid the dance they chanted forth a sacred song
Of Balder, of the pious god ; how he was loved
By every being ; how he fell before the shaft
Of Höder fell, and earth and ocean wept.[2] The song

Seemed not of mortal tone, nor sung by human voice;
But like a strain from Breidablick, home of the god;
Like song of lonely maid who thinks upon her lover,
When in the silent night the deep-toned quail pipes
     forth,
And the moon shineth o'er the birches in the North.
Frithiof stood charmed, supported by his sword, and
     gazed
Upon the dance; whilst childhood's mem'ries thronged
Before his eyes, an innocent and cheerful troop,
With eyes as blue as heaven, and with graceful heads
Streaming with curly golden hair; they lightly waved
A friendly greeting to their former youthful friend.
Then like a bloody shadow sank his viking life
With all its combats, struggles, and adventures wild,
Down into lower darkness, and his fancy saw
A flower-encircled monument above their tomb.
And as the song waxed loud, he lifted up his soul
From earth and earthly things to vaulted Valaskjalf;[3]
And man's revenge and hate now melted gently from
     him,
As from the mountain's breast melts the cuirass of ice
When shines the sun in spring. A sea of quiet joy,
Of silent rapture, poured into his hero-breast.
It was as if he felt the heart of Nature beat
Against his own; as if with passion he could press

The universe in brotherly embrace, and found
'Fore God a lasting peace with every living thing.
Then came into the temple Balder's great high-priest,
A lofty form, not like the god both young and fair,
But heavenly gentleness upon his features writ;
Whilst, sweeping to his belt, floated his silver beard.
Unusual veneration seized on Frithiof's soul,
The eagle plumes upon his helm were lowered deep
Before the priest; but he with friendly accent spoke:
" Son Frithiof, welcome hither !   I awaited thee;
For youth and strength must wander wild round earth
        and sea,
Like to the berserk[4] pale who hews the buckler's edge,
But tired of life and sobered, comes back home at last.
The mighty Thor went many a time to Jötunsheim;[5]
But yet, despite his belt divine and gloves of steel,
Utgarda Loké sitteth yet upon his throne;
Evil, itself a mighty force, yields not to force.
Goodness is nought but child's play uncombined with
        strength :
'Tis like the sunbeam bright upon the ocean's breast—
A fitful image, glittering in the inconstant wind,
Devoid of all consistence, for it hath no base.
But strength, devoid of piety, consumes itself,
E'en as the sword within the tomb; 'tis life's debauch,
Oblivion's heron hovers o'er the goblet's brim;

But when the drunkard wakes, he blushes for his deeds.

All strength is from the earth, derived from Ymer's[6]
    form;

The bois'trous waters are the veins which course therein,

And from the ore of mines are forged its sinews strong.

Yet desert are its plains, its spaces vast unfruitful,

Until the sun of piety doth shine thereon;

Then flourishes the grass, then blooms the purple flower,

The tree lifts up its head, and brings forth golden fruit,

And man and beast are nourished from their mother's
    breast.

So is it, too, with Asker's[7] child. The Almighty Father

Within the balance of our life hath placed two weights,

Which counterpoise each other, when the scale is true,

And earthly strength and heavenly piety their names.

Mighty indeed is Thor, young man, when, girding tight

His Megingjard[8] around his iron loins, he strikes.

Wise, too, is Odin, when in Urda's silver wave

He looketh down, and when the ravens flying come

Unto the Asa-sire with tidings of the world.

Yet dim became they both, the radiance of their
    crowns

Half-quenched when Balder, god of goodness, fell;

For he encircled was by Valhall's crown divine.

When yellow grew the summit of the tree of time,

And Nidhögg ate away its roots,[9] then were released

The powers of darkness, and the Midgard serpent
    struck
His matter-swollen tail 'gainst heaven, and Fenris howled[10]
And Surtur's[11] fiery sword flashed red from Muspelheim.
But now, where'er thine eye is cast, strife rages wild
With war-shield round the universe. In Valhall crowed
The cock with yellow comb; the blood-red cock of strife
Crowed upon earth and 'neath the earth. Before, 'twas
    peace,
Not only in the halls of heaven, but e'en on earth;
Peace reigned supreme in human and in godlike breasts;
For that which happens here already hath ta'en place
On more stupendous scale above. The universe
Is but a picture of Valhalla, as heaven's light
Mirrors itself upon the Saga's runic shield.
Each bosom hath its Balder. Think but of the time,
When peace abode within thy breast, when life was pure,
As glad and innocent as the wood-songster's dream,
When in the summer night the breezes gently wave
Each sleepy blossom's head upon its grassy bed;
Then Balder yet existed in thy pure young soul,
Thou Asa-son, thou image of Valhalla's gods !
God is not dead for children, and Hel renders up
His prey again whene'er a human being's born.
But side by side with Balder, in each human soul,
Grows his blind brother, Höder;[12] for all evil is

Born blind, as youthful bears are born, and dark Night
    is
Its cloak, for Goodness ever clothes itself in light,
Loké, the watchful tempter, constantly is there,
And guides blind Höder's murderous hand; and the
    slight shaft
Pierces Valhalla's darling, sinks into young Balder's
    heart.
Then Hate awoke, Oppression sprang upon his prey,
And hungry roamed the Wolf of Death round hill and
    dale,
And ships swam furiously upon the blood-stained sea;
For Piety sat powerless, like an empty shadow,
Dead amongst things extinct, in pallid Hel's abode;
And burnt to ashes now is Balder's sacred house.
Thus are the mighty Asas' lives a truthful image
Of fall'n humanity's condition; both are but
Allfather's silent meditations, and ne'er change.
What was, what will be, knows alone the Vala's[13] song.
That song is both Times's lullaby and funeral dirge.
The universe's annals tune themselves to this,
And each may hear in it his destiny unfolded.
Say, dost thou comprehend? The Vala questions thee.—

Thou wilt be reconciled. Know'st thou what this
    portends?

Look up into my face, young man, and wax not pale.
On earth a reconciler stalks—his name is *Death*.
All Time is from the first but stained eternity,
All Life a mean reflection from Allfather's throne ;
And pardon means to go back thither purified.
The mighty Asas fell themselves ; and Ragnarök
Their day of reconciliation, day of blood,
On Vigrid's drear and spacious plain ; on this they fall,
And yet they fall not unrevenged, for Evil dies
For ever ; but the Good which fell again arises
Up from the burning world, refined and purified.
The starry garlands bright fall pale and withered down
From heaven's temple, and the earth sinks deep in
  ocean,
But fairer still they rise again, and lift up glad
Their flower-encircled heads high from the ocean wave.
New stars and planets move above with godlike
  splendour,
And wend their quiet way over the new creation.
But o'er the verdant hill-tops, Balder gladly leads
The new-born Asas, and a race of men more pure.
The golden runic tables too, which once were lost
In Time's first dawn, by chance were found, hid in the
  grass,
On Ida's spacious plain, by Valhall's pardoned child.
Thus is the fall of Goodness but its fiery proof,

Its expiation ; born unto a better life,

It flieth back with spirit purged to whence it came,

E'en as a guileless child flies to its father's knee.—

Alas ! that all that's best should lie beyond the tomb,

That mound, green gate of Gimlé,[14] and that all is low,

And stained and tainted all that lies beneath the stars.

Yet e'en life may gain a reconciliation,

Inferior and a prelude to the higher one.

As when the skald, who runs his fingers o'er the harp

Ere he commence the wond'rous melody, with art

Touches the tuneful wires, and softly proves them till

Full harmony bursts powerful from the golden strings ;

Then charms he glorious mem'ries from forgotten graves,

And Valhall's radiance streams before the listener's eye.

For earth is but the shade of heaven, and life is but

The portico to Balder's temple in the sky.

The crowd adores the gods, and leads the charger forth,

Gold-saddled, purple-bridled, to the sacrifice.

This is a symbol, and of deep import, for blood

Is the red dawn of Reconciliation's day.

But symbols are not things and cannot aught effect,

And thy transgressions past thyself must expiate.

The dead are pardoned by Allfather's grace divine,

The quick must pardon find within the heart's recess.

I know an off'ring sweeter far to gods above,

Than sacrificial smoke, it is the off'ring of

The wild revenge and hate which rages in thy heart.
Can'st thou not mitigate their fury, can'st thou not
Forgive, young man, what dost thou here in Balder's
    house ?
What signifies the temple which thou here hast built ?
Balder is not appeased by stone ; with peace alone
Above as here below dwells reconciliation.
A Balder dwelt once in the South, a virgin's son,
Sent by Allfather to expound the mystic runes
Writ on the Nornas' sable shields, unknown before.
Peace was his war-cry, love to men his shining sword,
And Innocence sat dove-like on his silver helm.
Pious he lived and taught, until at last he died,
And 'neath far distant palms his grave in glory shines.
His doctrine, say they, spreadeth far from vale to vale,
Melteth the hardened heart and joins the friendly hand,
And founds the reign of peace upon the gladdened
    earth.
I know not well the creed indeed but darkly still
Have I in better hours had glimpses of his teaching,
At times each human heart yearns toward it, e'en as
    mine.
One day, I feel assured, it comes and lightly waves
Its snowy dove-like wings over the northern hills.
But ah ! no North will longer be for us that day,
The oak will sadly sigh o'er our forgotten graves.

Ye tribes more fortunate, who then will quench your
    thirst,
From the bright beaker filled with new-born light, I hail
    you !
Your fortune, if it chase away each cloud which hangs
Its damp, unwholesome shroud before the sun of life.
Likewise, despise us not, who honestly inquired
With unaverted eye for light and truth divine,
One is Allfather, many are his messengers.

" Thou hatest Belé's sons.   But wherefore hatest thou ?
Unto a simple freeman's son they have refused
To give their sister, for she is of Seming's blood,
The mighty son of Odin, whose heroic race
Counts their descent from Valhall's throne ; this causeth
    pride.
But noble birth is chance, and not desert, thou sayest.
Of his desert, young man, a man is never proud,
But of his fortune, and that surely is the best
Which is the gift of gods.   Art thou not proud thyself
Of thy heroic deeds, of thy superior force ?
Who gave thee thy great strength ? And did not Asa
    Thor
Knit thine arm's thews and sinews like an oaken branch?
Comes not from God the untamed heart which boundeth
    glad

Within the fortress of thy vaulted breast ?   And is
Not godlike lightning flashing from thy burning eye ?
The mighty Nornas by thy cradle chanted clear
The royal story of thy life ; and thy desert
Is not superior to the brothers' royal birth.
Judge not the pride of others, that thou be not judged.
"Now is King Helgé fallen."   Here broke Frithiof in :
"King Helgé fallen ?   When and where ?"   "Thou
          know'st thyself,
Whilst thou wast building here, he led an expedition
Against the mountain Finns.   Upon a craggy rock
Arose an aged temple, raised to Jumala.[15]
Now was it closèd and for many a year abandoned.
But high above the portal stood, famed far and wide,
An ancient statue of the god, inclined and tottering,
But no man durst approach it, for a saying went
Among the country folk, that who should haply first
Visit the temple, should behold the god Jumala.
This Helgé heard, and with blind, eager passion moved,
Sprang up the barren path against the hated god,
And would prostrate the temple.   When he reached the
          top,
The door was locked, the key was fixed by rust therein.
The doorposts then he seized, and wildly shook the
          frame
Of mouldering wood, when, with a fearful crash,

The statue fell to earth, and overwhelmed in falling
The son of Valhalla, and then he saw Jumala.
A midnight messenger hath brought these tidings hither.
Now Halfdan sits alone upon his father's throne;
Offer to him thy hand, and sacrifice revenge.
The off'ring Balder claims, I claim myself, his priest,
In token that ye jest not with the peaceful god.
If thou refusest, is the temple built in vain,
And vainly have I spoken."

                  Now stepped Halfdan in
Over the brazen threshold, and with wistful look
Stood silent, at a distance from the dreaded one.
Then Frithiof loosed the Harness-hater from his thigh,
Against the altar placed the golden buckler round,
And forward came unarmed to meet his enemy :
"In such a strife," thus he commenced, with friendly
      voice,
"The noblest he who first extends the hand of peace."
Then blushed King Halfdan deep, and drew his gauntlet
      off,
And long-divided hands now firmly clasped each other,
A mighty pressure, steadfast as the mountain's base.
The old man then absolved him from the curse which
      lay
Upon the Varg i Veum,[16] on the outlawed man.
And as he spake the words, fair Ingeborg came in,

Arrayed in bridal dress, and followed by fair maids,
E'en as the stars escort the moon in heaven's vault.
Whilst tears suffused her soft and lovely eyes, she fell
Into her brother's arms, but deeply moved he led
His cherished sister unto Frithiof's faithful breast,
And o'er the altar of the god she gave her hand
Unto her childhood's friend, the darling of her heart.

NOTES.

[1] Freya, the Scandinavian goddess of Love.

[2] Referring to the Runic or ancient Scandinavian alphabet.

[3] Valhalla: literally, "Abode of the chosen." Only the brave were admitted, after death, as companions of Odin. The Valkyrias, who in some measure correspond to the Houris of Eastern mythology, were supposed to hover over a battle-field and "elect" the most intrepid heroes; hence their name, connected with the German wählen and küren.

[4] Iduna, the Hebe of Scandinavian mythology.

[5] Frigga, the wife of Odin.

[6] Gerda, a beautiful giant maiden, with whom Frey, the god of Fertility, was enamoured.

[7] Nanna, the emblem of feminine love and tenderness, wife of Balder, one of the chief Scandinavian divinities, of whom more below.

[8] Balder, the symbol of all that is good and holy in the universe. His death was the signal for the reign of Evil. It occurred in the following manner. Balder was troubled by evil dreams; so, in a council of the gods, it was resolved that Frigga should exact an oath from all substances that they would do no harm to Balder. This being done the gods, in their joy, proved his invulnerability by slashing at him, throwing stones, and shooting arrows. Loké, the evil spirit, envious of the honours accorded to Balder, came and asked Frigga if all nature had sworn to do no harm to Balder; she replied that all had, with the exception of a plant in Valhalla, called "mistletoe." Loke, on hearing this,

immediately went and plucked some mistletoe, and, returning
to the council, asked his blind brother, Höder, why he also did
not shoot at Balder.   On his excusing himself on the score of
his blindness, Loké placed the mistletoe in his hand, and directed the shot, which pierced the bosom of Balder, who fell
dead, to the consternation of the assembled gods.   Balder, on his
death, descended to Helheim, the abode of Evil.   The perpetua-
tion of the use of the mistletoe at Christmas is curious.   Doubt-
less, on the introduction of Christianity into the North, the
Romish priests represented Christ as identical with Balder; and
thus the instrument of the latter's death has been handed down
to us even as the cross has been.

⁹ Odin, the chief divinity of the Scandinavians.   He is termed
" All-father," " Father of the gods," " The mighty," " The prudent and circumspect," &c., &c.   He is represented as bearing a
spear or javelin, which always struck its mark, Gungnir, *i.e.*, the
earthquake, and a ring, the emblem of eternity.

¹⁰ Thor, the god of Truth and Strength.   He was " the strongest
of all the gods," and his attribute was Mjölnir, the hammer,
which always hit the mark and returned of itself to Thor's hand.
" Mjölnir " signifies the " Shatterer," to indicate the crushing
force of truth.

¹¹ Thrudvang, the abode of Thor, signifying " The home of
Truth and Strength."

II.

¹ Odin was accompanied by two ravens, who whispered in his
ear tidings of the world.

² A portion of the Elder Edda.

³ *Vide* note I. 6.

III.

¹ Bragè, or Bragi, " The Speaker," the god of music, poetry,
and oratory.

² The well or spring Mimer was, in Northern mythology, the
symbol of knowledge and experience.

[3] It must be remembered that the Gothic races came originally from the East.

[4] One of the Nornas, or Fates.

[5] Frey, the god of fertility, is often symbolised as the Sun.

[6] Saga, the muse of history.

[7] Hel, the ruler of Niflheim, the abode of cowards after death.

[8] Glitnir, the " Shining," was the abode of Forseti, son of Balder and Nanna, and the personification of Justice.

[9] The sea-god.

IV.

[1] *Vide* III. 7.

[2] Frithiof is supposed to be an " odalbonde," or allodial proprietor.

VII.

[1] Delling, the father of the Sun.

[2] *Vide* note I. 3.

[3] The abode of Freya, goddess of Love.

[4] Ragnarök, the burning of the world. On this day the Asas, or gods, are attacked and destroyed by the powers of darkness, the world is consumed by fire and sunk beneath the sea, from which, however, it arises renovated. The Asas are then restored to a purified existence, and Balder is released from the power of Hel; the reign of Evil, which had commenced at his death, having perished for ever.

VIII.

[1] The well by which dwelt the three Nornas, or Fates : Urda, Verdandi, and Skulda.

[2] Gefion, a goddess, to whom all virgins, who died as such, went after death.

[3] The rainbow, supposed to be a bridge between heaven and earth.

[4] Asa is the name for the Scandinavian gods.

[5] The Nornas were, as has been before mentioned, the Fates or Destinies; one was supposed to attend on each individual during life.

[6] A "Vala," or "Völva," signifies a woman who foretells the future. Odin is related to have consulted the deceased Vala about the death of Balder, and by the employment of strange exorcisms to have obtained a full response.

[7] Niding, according to Fritzner's "Icelandic-Danish Dictionary," a person who disgraces himself by shameful actions, and especially a traitor.

[8] Slidur, a miry stream which flowed through Helheim.

[9] See note 6.

X.

[1] Rana, a sea-goddess, supposed to catch those who fell into the sea in her net. She was married to Œgir, the sea-god, and had nine daughters, personifying the waves.

XI.

[1] Berserk, according to Fritzner's Icelandic-Danish Dictionary, "A man who, at times, but especially in combat, is wont to be seized with a wild, animal fury, which gives him extraordinary strength, and makes his assault almost irresistible." Akin to the "ghazee" of Eastern climes, except that the "wild, animal fury" of the latter is produced by opium.

[2] *Vide* III. 6.

[3] *Vide* III. 2.

[4] Name of a fairy.

XII.

[1] Œgir's daughter, *i.e.*, the waves; *vide* X. 1.

[2] Loké; *vide* I. 8. It will be remembered that he appeared at

the assembly of the gods as an old woman previous to Balder's death.

[3] Var, goddess of oaths.

[4] Vidar, the personification of Immortality. He dwells in primæval forests, and is termed "the Silent."

[5] Lofn, goddess of marriage.

XIII.

[1] The Aurora Borealis.

[2] Höder, brother to Lokó; he is represented blind, and is the symbol of Darkness.

[3] A symbol of strife and destruction.

[4] The flames. Muspelheim was a burning world, guarded by Surtur with a flaming sword.

XIV.

[1] Rana; *vide* X. 1.

[2] Cowards were placed in the stocks on the judgment-day.

[3] *Vide* III. 6.

XVII.

[1] The Einheris were the warriors of Valhalla.

XVIII.

[1] Sleipnir, Odin's white and *eight*-legged horse.

XIX.

[1] Nastrand, *i.e.*, Niflheim, the abode of Hel.

[2] Temple-ravisher : literally, " Wolf in sanctuaries.'

XXI.

[1] Bifrost. *Vide* VIII. 3.
[2] A name for Freya.
[3] *Vide* III. 6.
[4] *Vide* III. 8.
[5] Poetical names for gold.

XXII.

[1] The Nornas were termed " Sköldemör," or " Shield-maidens."
[2] The ash tree, Yggdrafill, was the symbol of the history of the world. Its roots are three-fold : one directed towards the gods, the second to empty space, and the third to Niflheim. Near the first dwell the Nornas, Urda, Verdandi, and Skulda; near the second is the well Mimer; and under the third lies the serpent Nidhögg, who constantly gnaws the root of the ash. Nidhögg is the symbol of death.

XXIII.

[1] *Vide* XXII. 2.
[2] Breidablick, the abode of Balder.

XXIV.

[1] Parts of the Elder Edda, an Icelandic collection of epic poems.
[2] *Vide* I. 8.
[3] Valaskjalf, the vaulted abode of Odin.
[4] *Vide* XL. 1.
[5] The abode of the giants.
[6] A giant, from whose substance the earth was made.
[7] Askr and Embla, two trees found lifeless by the gods, who endowed them with the qualities which constituted them the progenitors of the human race.
[8] Thor's belt of strength.

9 *Vide* XXII. 2.

10 Fenrir, the "Wolf of Death," who slew Odin on the day of Ragnarök. *Vide* VII. 4.

11 Surtur, the guardian of Muspelheim. He was armed with a flaming sword, and burnt the world at Ragnarök. *Vide* XIII. 4.

12 *Vide* I. 8.

13 *Vide* VIII. 6.

14 A name for Heaven.

15 A Finnish god.

16 *Vide* XIX. 2.

THE END.

BRADBURY, EVANS, AND CO., PRINTERS, WHITEFRIARS.

www.ingramcontent.com/pod-product-compliance
Lightning Source LLC
Chambersburg PA
CBHW020616030726
47497CB00007B/2276